Firepower

JOHN
CUTTER
FIREPOWER

A VINCE BELLATOR THRILLER

LUME BOOKS

LUME BOOKS

Published in 2021 by Lume Books
30 Great Guildford Street,
Borough, SE1 0HS

ISBN 978-1-83901-212-9

Typeset using Atomik ePublisher from Easypress Technologies

www.lumebooks.co.uk

ABOUT THE AUTHOR

John Cutter is the author of the Specialist novels. He and his wife live in Washington State, USA, with three dogs and a growing rock'n'roll collection vinyl-record collection.

To Jack Sullivan

CHAPTER ONE

When Vince Bellator first heard the rattle of gunfire, he figured it was hunters. Out of an old combat reflex, he assessed the source, making it about a quarter mile southeast. It was early October, a sweet-smelling dusk in Southern Appalachia, and Vince figured he was hearing a sample of the local deer-hunting season.

Wearing a brown leather WW2 vintage pilot's jacket, a green army t-shirt and hiking boots, Vince had started the hike in the Blue Ridge mountains a few days before. He'd worked his way down into northern Alabama, camped in Cheaha State Park in Alabama last night. But this morning he'd trekked out of the state park, onto the big federal forest reserve, and he'd done it on purpose. Vince wanted solitude.

Vince was thirty-three years old, in good shape, having no trouble with the full backpack and no fear of the wilderness. An Army Ranger and Delta Force operative till three years ago, he'd always aced wilderness training.

A few more gunshots sounded. No problem, easy enough to avoid the hunters. But then he heard quite another gun—this time the unmistakable rattle of machine gunfire. He knew from the sound it was a Browning M2—a classic weapon. If they were using that for elk hunting, there wouldn't be much left of the animal.

He heard the machine gun rattle again and decided it wasn't hunters after all. Could be automatic-weapon enthusiasts, maybe moneyed wannabes selling access to a machine gun. Gun-fun, under the radar. They were chewing up some target, likely a tree stump, with fairly expensive rounds. After a minute, a breeze from that direction brought him the distinctive smell of the .50 caliber ammo. He smelled something else that surprised him. Tracer ammo had a particular odor of its own. Why were these guys using tracer bullets? It was dusk, not night, and the bright tracer streaks wouldn't shine out.

Vince's route would take him fairly close to the firing range. He was heading through the Talladega National Forest, on his way to a lonely place outside the preserve; a spot called Dead Springs, where he expected to find no one at all—nothing but an empty cabin. It was a place that a comrade-in-arms had asked him to visit, to 'take care of a little job for me'. And in fact, Chris Destry had been dying in Vince's arms when he asked him to bury a certain something at the cabin.

Striding along the scant trail, his boots crackling in the first layer of fallen leaves, Vince heard another long strafe of gunfire, a little closer now. He shrugged; he could skirt away from the gunners, whoever they were, when he got a little closer. He'd still find the cabin. He had a reliable sense of direction.

Another four hundred yards along the ridgetop, as the shadows of the oaks and longleaf pines stretched out to crisscross the thin trail, Vince began to hear the faint sounds of men's voices. The gun enthusiasts. Too far to hear what they were saying.

A glimmer caught his attention, high in a pine tree nearby. He made out a lens up there, flashing in the failing light from the west. A camera. Was that some kind of wildlife observation cam? Or something else?

He was aware that he was not here legally; he'd soon be crossing into private land belonging to Chris's family to go to the cabin, but right now he was still in a National Forest preserve. Not supposed to just wander around here without permission, though that was just what he was doing. Too bad the camera had caught him there. No big deal; if he ran into a forest ranger of some kind, he'd pay a fine and move on.

It was about time to leave the trail, anyway, circle off to the northwest to avoid the gun range. He looked for a good place to cut into the woods—then became aware that someone was coming up the slope toward him, off to the right. He could hear them pushing clumsily through underbrush, grunting with effort. Sounded like three men.

He thought about ducking into the underbrush to avoid them. But he was still on National Forest land. These guys didn't sound like rangers. Nor was this their private property—they didn't own the land any more than he did. Did they even have permission to put up those cameras?

Better have a look at them. He instinctively wanted to know who was in the area. These guys were within a couple miles of Dead Springs, which was where he planned to spend the night.

Vince shrugged out of his backpack and leaned it against a pine trunk. Best to be unencumbered when encountering strangers in a remote area.

He waited, and then the three men came puffing up onto the

trail and came to a stop about twenty feet away, staring at him. They were all wearing paramilitary garb—and they all carried AR-15 rifles.

"Well there he is," said the shorter of the three men, "big as life." He wore a paramilitary cap, half covering his short blond hair.

"He's a big dude, alright," said the pudgy, red-faced man beside him. There was a certain swagger in their banter that Vince attributed to the AR-15s. Carrying automatic weapons made some people feel powerful.

The short guy and pudgy one had the same type of cap, the same cammies, unmarked by any insignia. The third man said nothing. He was darker, deeply tanned, black hair, no cap, lips pursed in his craggy, pocked face. He had the stripes of a master sergeant on his cammie jacket. But apart from the marks of rank, no insignia. All three men had their fatigues tucked into military-issue boots. Were they from some kind of National Guard training program? But they would have the insignia for that.

"Ya'll are trespassing," said the pudgy man.

"This is the Talladega National Forest, isn't it?" Vince asked calmly.

The man blinked and shuffled his feet. "*Ye*-es. But this trail is right on the edge of private property. And it's not an authorized trail."

"You work for the US Forest service?"

"Well—no."

"You have some kind of special permission to be here yourselves?" Vince made it sound as if he was just curious.

The big man with the sergeant's stripes answered for pudgy guy. "That's not at issue." He had a deep, rumbling voice. "We belong here. You don't. We saw you on security camera; we came to tell you to turn back."

"That a federal security camera?" Vince asked, as if only casually interested.

The sergeant frowned. "Doesn't matter whose it is."

"Colls, I don't think this guy gets it," said the short guy with the blond hair, talking to the sergeant.

"Don't use my name in the field without authorization," growled Colls, glaring at the shorter man. "And you address me as Sergeant."

"Okay, fine—what we going to do about the intruder, Sergeant?"

"I'm just passing through," Vince said. "I'm on my way to private land. I have permission to camp there. I came from this direction because I wanted to see the Talladega forest. If you boys can move out of the way, I'll head on."

Colls shook his head and hefted the AR-15. "You're not passing through here. You're going back the way you came. You find some other route to where you're going. But not in this forest. Not at all."

"You going to use that rifle on me if I don't go back the way I came?" Vince asked. He had no gun himself, not with him. Just a razor-sharp army-issue combat knife, neither too big nor too small, in a metal sheath on his right hip. It had served him well on a number of night missions.

"I don't think that will be necessary," said Colls. "We'll use our rifles only on assigned targets, or in self-defense. There's three of us. You'll go, alright."

"'Assigned targets'? You fellas have regulations and everything! Nice and shiny. Who are you… serving with?"

"We'll ask the questions," said the red-faced guy, stepping forward, now jabbing the AR-15 toward Vince. "Sarge, what if he's FBI?"

Colls grunted. "Not impossible." He scowled at Vince. "What's your name?"

"What's yours—I mean, besides Colls?" Vince asked. "I'll show you my ID if you show me yours. All I have is a driver's license." He smiled sadly at the pudgy guy. "I'm afraid I'm not with the FBI. Nothing so interesting. I'm an out of work freelancer, taking a hike." The concern about the FBI reinforced Vince's suspicion that these men were from some off-brand militia.

"Just show me your ID," Colls said, pointing the rifle at Vince. "Now."

Vince gave them a faint smile. Inside, he was taut, feeling anger build. He didn't like anyone to point a gun at him. Ever.

But he stretched, as if loose and bored, then shrugged and said, "I guess I'll have to revise my plan." He looked at the AR-15 in the hands of the nearer, red-faced man. "That's a nice new weapon you've got. Selective fire?" Smiling, Vince took a couple steps toward the pudgy man, keeping the militiaman between himself and the other two, as if he wanted to admire the gun. He noticed pudgy guy hadn't taken the safety off on his rifle. "What load you use?"

"Stop right there!" Colls growled. "Give me your ID and then put your hands up!"

Vince shrugged. "Sure thing." He reached into a pocket, slowly, so as not to make the militiamen nervous, and drew out a wallet. There was very little in the wallet. It was slim. It contained a Veterans Administration card, a driver's license, and a thousand dollars in cash. No credit cards. Nothing else.

He took out the driver's license, replaced his wallet, humming "Strangers in the Night" as he did it—and suddenly skimmed the plastic-encased license at Colls' feet. The three strangers automatically looked at it.

Colls bent to pick it up—and Vince made a series of moves in under two seconds.

Vince stepped in close to the pudgy guy, grabbing the barrel of the AR-15, jerking it from the militiaman's hands before he could move, instantaneously ramming it back into the man's gut. Pudgy guy gasped and bent double. With one hand, Vince reversed the AR-15. With the other, he grabbed pudgy guy by the neck and dragged him up to block the muzzle of the short guy who was trying to move into a firing position.

The militia sergeant was straightening up, the license in one hand, rifle in the other. Neither he nor the short guy could hit Vince from where they were without killing their buddy.

"Freeze!" Vince snarled.

He had the rifle pointing at the sergeant, its stock braced on his hip, his finger on the trigger. He hadn't had time to take the safety off too—but he figured they weren't going to see that from where they were.

The pudgy guy was wheezing, Vince's hand tight on his throat, hopelessly trying to claw away the hand that choked him. His face was turning scarlet.

The short blond guy was gaping at Vince.

"You tell me your name—your real name—and I'll let you three live," Vince told him.

"Shaun Adler!" the short guy blurted.

"Dammit, Shaun!" Colls snapped.

"And the other two, Shaun?"

"Mac Colls and Wynn Foster!"

"Goddamn you, Adler!" Colls roared.

"Now drop your gun," said Vince. "You too, Sergeant. Do what I say and you can all walk away. Fail, and I'll cut you three down like weeds. I've killed enough men, it'll come easy."

Adler dropped his gun.

Licking his lips, Colls looked into Vince's eyes—then he took a long breath—and angrily tossed his own rifle aside.

Vince shoved Foster into the short guy so they both fell backwards, one atop the other.

"Now what?" Colls growled, and the two other militiamen untangled and got gasping to their feet.

Vince took the AR-15 into both hands, leveling it at Colls from waist height. Almost as an afterthought, he flicked off the safety. He knew by the weight of the gun that it was loaded. "Now," Vince said, "this."

He swung the muzzle of the gun a couple inches over and squeezed the trigger, sending a short burst into the dirt of the trail between Colls and the two men.

"Yah-h-h!" wailed Foster as he turned and bolted into the forest to Vince's right.

The other two raised their hands. "Don't shoot!" Adler squeaked.

Vince grinned. "I just did!" He nodded toward his driver's license, still in Colls' left hand. "Sergeant, lay that on the trail there. Then you take Shaun here and follow Foster off into the brush. Go on back to shooting your playthings at targets. And don't fuck with me ever again."

"What about our weapons?" Colls asked, putting the driver's license on the ground.

"I'll wreck two of them. I'll keep the third. I'm going to be moving fast and carefully through the brush. You won't be able to track me. If you come looking for me, I'll nail you."

Between grating teeth, Colls said, "You don't know who you're fucking with!"

"I truly do not care who you are. I mind my own business, whenever I can. Chalk the loss of your weapons off to the learning curve." He raised the rifle to his shoulder and pointed it at Colls' head. "You've got a two count. One…"

Colls turned and strode off to Vince's right, into the brush, Adler scrambling after him.

Vince went to the verge of the slope and peered down through the underbrush. He could see Colls and Adler half sliding, scrambling down the hillside.

Vince removed the ammo from two of the rifles then smashed the weapons against a granite outcropping till they were unusable and beyond repair.

He picked up the intact rifle, his license, and his backpack, and headed off into the deepening shadow of the brush, making his roundabout way toward Dead Springs.

"What did you get off his driver's license?" Gustafson asked.

Colls handed him a sheet of paper with the info written on it. "Wasn't time to get a lot of it, sir. His name is Vincent J. Bellator. Residence is given as Harstine Island, Washington State. I didn't have time to get the street address but how many Vincent J. Bellators could there be on some island in Washington?"

Raoul Gustafson nodded as he looked at the paper, his coke bottle-lens glasses flashing in the caged overhead light of the bunker. A stocky, middle-aged man, he wore paramilitary desert cammies, and on his shoulders were a general's four stars. "Vincent Jack *Bellator?* Do you know that Bellator is Latin for *warrior?*"

Colls shook his head. He wasn't surprised that Raoul knew it. Gustafson had a PhD. He'd been a professor, but they'd booted him out of the post for Holocaust denialism.

"I'll run it past my contact in the State Department. He'll get this man's records. We'll find out soon enough if he's a federal agent of some kind."

The two men were standing in Gustafson's small Operations Office in the Germanic Brethren bunker complex. The entrance of the Wolf Base complex was a mile from the border of the Talladega reserve. Mostly subterranean—built into the side of a steel granite ridge—the complex rose at the center of Gustafson's four hundred-acre property.

A man with $180 million of inherited tobacco money to spend, Gustafson had given the complex every relevant amenity. Barracks with showers and latrines, air conditioning and central heating, well-stocked kitchens, extensive storerooms for food and munitions and medical supplies, an armory, a basement brig, and high-powered communications gear that kept him in touch with Brethren cells around the country.

Gustafson turned away, going down the hall to the comm room, calling out, "Sit down, have some coffee if you want, and wait for orders, Mac."

Mackenzie Colls didn't feel like sitting—he was too tense, too angry. But the habit of obedience to General Gustafson was strong, and he sat in the creaking gray-metal folding chair in front of the oak desk.

Quietly fuming, Mac Colls went over the incident again in his mind. Bellator had humiliated Colls and his patrol detail. The others were the weaker elements of the Brethren, and perhaps they deserved it. But Colls was a seasoned soldier. He was a former Marine; he'd fought in the Iraq war. He'd received a bronze star and two purple hearts. It was true he'd been dishonorable discharged—but that was all part of the conspiracy against him. When they'd found out he had let his men use "enhanced inter-rogation" on the suspected Al Qaeda operative and, indeed, had executed the man himself to shut him up, the MPs jumped at the chance to get rid of him. They knew his feelings about Densmore, the black captain who so blithely ordered Colls around. Mac Colls had worked hard to put together a platoon of white national-ists—and Captain Densmore had broken it up.

Never again, he'd vowed, after his discharge, would he bear a humiliation from an enemy of the cause. He could barely stay in his seat now; he was itching for orders to find this Bellator and kill him.

Still, whatever Gustafson's orders were, Colls would follow them. Gustafson had found Colls on the streets in Atlanta, living in an old Buick LeSabre, drunk and angry and aimless. The general had given him a new life, a new direction. Colls had been waiting for a leader, a true believer like Raoul Gustafson, all his life. General Gustafson was the man to lead the Brethren in the coming race war.

The fifty-man core Brethren had been training for seven years. Thanks to an online recruitment drive, they'd doubled their ranks. It was true they had a good many amateurs among the new men—like Foster and Adler. He'd only taken those two with him today, when he saw the hiker on the security video, to give them a chance to engage in a routine detail. Now and then he had to turn away some hiker or a homeless person looking for a place to hide in the forest. He'd expected no trouble. The General quietly paid off a couple of Forest Service men responsible for this part of the forest, and whatever the Brethren wanted was okay, long as they were careful about fire safety.

But Bellator had been a surprise...

There was something about the man. Something quietly dangerous. Like an IED he'd see exposed on the roadside, back in Iraq. It was just there, a motionless tangle of wires around a plastic explosive packet—waiting to explode.

The minutes passed as Mac Colls fidgeted in the hard chair. He thought about getting that cup of coffee.

But then Gustafson came out of the comm room, his wide, froggish face creased by a frown. He tossed a print-out onto his desk. "Look at that. I was able to obtain a file on Bellator. Our man in the Pentagon gave us what he could. That the man you encountered?"

Colls opened the folder and looked at the computer-printed color photo. "That's him, sir. That's the man."

The General sat at his desk and tented his fingers. "My man had the goods on your troublemaker. Bellator is a Yale grad, Phi Beta Kappa. Multi-athletic. Big in college triathlons. Joined the Army Rangers, took officer's training, made lieutenant. Fought in Afghanistan. Double handful of medals. Made captain. Then he transferred to Delta Force..."

"Delta Force! Holy shit—sir."

"Yes. His time in Delta Force is classified and we don't know what he did for them, except some of it was in Iraq, some in Somalia, and some of it was Syria, and there was one secret mission to Pakistan. There were other missions where no location is given. Then his time's done, he decides not to re-up. But the feds keep track of him. He hires on with an outfit called Pro-Active Security International. Kind of a Blackwater type situation. That went south and he quit the company. He's spent the last two years building a big house on that island in the Puget Sound, on property left to him by…" He looked at the file. "One 'Jack Sullivan'. An associate of his father's." General Gustafson shook his head. "This man Bellator is *deadly*. You boys got off easy! The CIA codename for him was *Charon*. You know who Charon is, Mac?"

"No sir."

"In Greek myths, he's the boatman who takes you to Hell."

Mac grunted. Vincent Bellator had seemed a normal man—big, yes, but not extraordinary. Not at first. He had short, dark brown hair, a lean square-jawed face weathered by a lot of time spent outdoors. During the whole encounter he'd seemed detached, mildly amused.

But Colls' mouth went dry as he remembered looking into Bellator's eyes once Vince got the AR-15 in his hands. Death had been waiting in those chilly gray eyes.

You can live or die, it's your call. That was the message he'd read there.

Colls shrugged. He wasn't going to let the son of a bitch intimidate him. "Sir—we can still kill him. He doesn't have to see it coming."

"Kill him? Not unless we have to! Mac, I don't want to kill Vincent Bellator. I want to recruit him!"

CHAPTER TWO

Katydids called stridently through the velvety night as Vince finished his hike in a fading Indian Summer warmth, passing through a grove of pine trees to Dead Springs. Approaching the clearing at the base of a low hill, he wasn't surprised to see Chris's mother, Rose Destry, sitting on the porch of the old cabin. She was hunched on the deck of the roofed front porch, her feet on the ground, in a pool of light from the lantern hanging overhead. They'd never met, but they'd talked on the phone, and he had seen pictures of her that Chris had shown to him.

They'd arranged to meet today—but he was a little disconcerted to find her here already. He was going to be burying one of Chris's body parts here. How was his mother going to feel about that? He was self-conscious about the AR-15 he carried on a strap over his right shoulder, too.

"Rose!" he said, stepping out into the thin moonlight. She sat up and squinted his way. "It's Vince Bellator."

"Vincent!" She stood up, smiling. "Come on to the cabin!"

He walked by the Dodge Ram extended-cab pickup parked to his right and joined her in the lantern light.

They looked each other over. She was a short, plump woman in blue jeans and a black and gray plaid shirt, untucked. Her long copper-colored hair, streaked with gray, hung behind her in double braids. There were old smile lines on her round face that were creasing toward sadness now. Her blue eyes had sparkled in photos; now they seemed flat with pain. She glanced at the AR-15 and he could see her decide not to ask about it yet.

She smiled ruefully at Vince. "I had no idea you were so... How tall are you?"

"Six-five."

"Lord, I thought my Chris was tall..." Her lips buckled and she turned away. "Come on. Have a drink and tell me all about it..."

She led the way into the cabin. It was three rooms, one story, rough-cut lacquered pine with interlocking corners. Judging by wear and tear, Vince guessed it had been built in the 1960s. Two battery-powered lanterns hung in the main room and a small wood fire burned in the stone hearth. A dusty elkhorn rack was poised over the fireplace. There was an old settee, one leg replaced by a chunk of firewood, across from a sofa, with a deeply worn hook rug between.

"Take the sofa, good for the big guys," she said, going to a little portable liquor cabinet that stood on wheels against the log wall.

Vince took off his pack, leaned it with the rifle against the wall, and sat back on the old faded-red sofa, feeling awkward. He glanced at the backpack and thought about what was in it. She didn't know about that.

"How about a whiskey and soda, Vincent? Got some Jameson here."

"That'll be fine."

15

"There's no electricity but I still have some ice that hasn't melted… Got a bag from the Quickie store down the road…" Her voice quavered a little. She seemed to be talking just to keep from crying. "The water's on, though; we have a tank-full. Not that much, but you can take a shower, get some cooking water, use the toilet. There's a septic tank. I put some food in the cooler—it's in the bedroom. Place doesn't have a kitchen to speak of, just a shed attached to the back with a sink. But you'll find a propane camp stove out there, pans, dishes, a coffee pot… and two pounds of coffee."

"It's… good of you to let me stay here for a few days," he said. "Chris always said we'd come out here and…" He winced. Probably not the right time to bring up what Chris would never again do. "…and do some fishing."

She brought him the drink, a tumbler with crushed ice, whiskey, a splash of soda, then sank down on the settee. She took a sip from her tumbler and said, "You can still do that, on your own. Fishing's at Chickasaw Creek, down the trail southwest. Dead Springs creek here, when it's running, empties into it. The spring runs when it's been raining, mostly… Supposedly called Dead Springs because most every time the hunters came here for a drink it was dry… There's been a couple days' rain, so it's got some ditchwater in it…"

They were silent for a minute. It seemed much longer than a minute. She gazed at the fire.

Vince could see unshed tears glistening in her eyes. She'd asked to meet him in person because he'd been with Chris when he'd died. "Rose—you still want to know how it happened? What happened to Chris? I mean—in more detail than 'a missile impact'?"

She looked at him. Firelight played on the left side of her face in the semi-lit room. "Yes. Please."

He nodded. He'd been hoping to spare her the hard fact that Chris had not died instantly. "We were in the Yucatan, in the jungle, that much you know. Just about twenty clicks from the border with Guatemala."

"What was that company called? He told me, and I even wrote to them once, but I seem to be blocking it…"

"Pro-Active Security International. PASI."

Rose shook her head sadly. "Not even the US military. To die working for people like that…"

Vince nodded. "I know what you mean. I'll just say—we were genuinely fighting bad guys. Enemies of America. The drug cartels. We had some connections to the DEA and Mexican State Security. We were subcontractors but…" He didn't want to go into it any farther. The campaign against the Yucatan cocaine and meth manufacturing centers had seemed to make sense to him. But it went sideways. Chris died because of PASI admin's sloppy intel and bad decisions. Then Vince heard about Tac Two's mission. Innocent people were killed. An entire family. Because PASI didn't care about the non-combatants. When Vince found out, he resigned from PASI. The PASI CFO said he was in violation of contract and refused to pay him the second 100k they owed him. But Vince didn't care. The job had already gone sour for him when Chris was killed. Now they were letting their men cut down innocent bystanders. He didn't want another cent from them.

Chris Destry and he were tight. Chris was a buddy who'd fought at Vince's side for three years in northern Afghanistan and two years in Delta Force.

He took a deep breath and went on. "We were about a quarter klick south of the factory and they must've gotten some sense of our heli insert—they sent out a drone to locate us. We spotted the drone watching us and I told PASI on the sat-link that we were burned, we should cancel the action. They insisted that the factory had no strong defenses and we had to go on. I was only in nominal command—mercenaries aren't bound by military law—so I asked the other men what they wanted to do. Every man wanted to go in, including Chris. There would be a big bonus if we took this dope factory down. So… I split the men into two teams, sent them at the factory in a double flank… but then the gunship came. They had their own second-hand Blackhawk—something we had no intel on. It was equipped with Air-to-Surface Missiles. We took cover but you don't get much shelter from missiles behind a tree. They let loose with four Tomahawks. I had an RPG-7—a shoulder-fired missile. We were going to use it on their comm center. I used it on the Blackhawk and it went down. I went to find Chris—he was most the way gone when I found him, about twenty-five meters off. He hadn't taken a direct hit but… he caught splash damage, lost his right hand and…" Vince cleared his throat. Suddenly his voice was getting hoarse. "…and, uh… received serious internal injuries from shrapnel. I got some morphine into him. We had about a minute to talk. I held him in my arms. Chis knew he was going. He didn't seem scared. He asked me to come here, to this cabin, do something for him… I said I would… Told me how to find it, asked me to tell you what happened, then he…" He swallowed hard. "Then he passed, Rose."

She hunched over, silently weeping, biting her lower lip, her eyes squeezed shut. Her drink slopped over, some splashing on the floor, the glass still clenched in her trembling hand.

Acting on instinct, Vince put his drink down and went to sit by Rose, his arm around her shoulders. He let her cry.

After a few minutes she sat up and took a long, ragged breath. She pulled a kerchief from her shirt pocket and wiped her eyes, then reached up and squeezed his hand. "Thank you, Vincent. You go on and… drink your drink. I'm okay."

"Yes ma'am."

Vince got up, having to clear his throat again, and returned to the sofa. He took a pull on the whiskey and soda. He didn't usually drink hard liquor but it went down well right then. "I guess you know how I felt about Chris—I told you in the email. But… I wasn't making a speech, Rose. I meant it. I've never served with a better man. He saved my life in Afghanistan. And he was… he was decent. The local people always liked him. When we were in Syria with Delta Force—he practically adopted a whole family. They were running on foot when the Syrian Army was coming in… He got them food and medicine and transportation. Talked a major into it, face to face. Risked his career to do that."

She nodded. "That was very Chris."

"Yes. That was Chris all the way."

"Where you from, Vincent? Chris must've told me, but I haven't slept much lately."

"Texas, ma'am. Out west of Amarillo."

"Chris said your dad was a military man too…"

"Two tours in Vietnam. Some… freelance work. Saved up his money and bought a farm. Him and Mama started a flower farm. For florists. That… and goats. They made it all work together."

"Flowers and goats? When you said Texas, I was expecting a cattle ranch."

19

He noticed her looking at the AR-15. "I guess you're wondering about me toting the semi-auto rifle out here…"

"I've seen people in this part of the country use them to hunt."

He shook his head. "I don't hunt unless I've got no other way to get something to eat. I took it off some knuckleheads in the Talladega. They tried to roust me."

"You… took it?"

He shrugged. "They were careless. Yeah. They're fine. I just disarmed them. Guys in paramilitary togs. Looked like militia. You know 'em?"

She snorted. "You had it right—knuckleheads. Dangerous ones. Germanic Brethren, they call themselves." She took a long pull at her drink. "You know I've got… had… two sons, right?"

"Sure. There's Bobby, Chris's younger brother. I saw some pictures. How's he doing?"

Rose looked into the fire and shook her head. "I really don't know. He's… It's funny you running into the Brethren. He got tangled up with those people. Believed a lot of lies they put on the internet and started hanging out with some men from the Wolf Base and… then he heard they were planning some kind of attack. Right here in the USA. He started doubting them. Realized they were lying when they… well, all the claims they made." Her eyes were still closed. "And he didn't want any part of it. Said he was going to resign from it. I told him not to go there again, even for that. But he insisted. He has a friend there he wanted to talk to." She shook her head. "I haven't heard from him since."

She pressed her lips together and stood up, went to refill her drink. "I swear I'm not going to cry again. And I'm not."

He heard the clink and swish of the drink being made, and

then she returned to the settee as Vince asked, "How long's it been since you heard from Bobby?"

"Six weeks. He's not answering his phone. Doesn't respond to texts. None of his friends have heard from him."

"Did you talk to the police?"

"They just shrugged it off. Said he was an adult and probably went off on his own."

"Could be he went dark because he was afraid of the militia. Didn't want you to be involved."

"Not like him to…" She took a drink, shuddered, and went on. "…to not be in touch at all. I'm so scared they've… *done* something to him. I was so shocked when he got involved with them. We didn't raise our kids to be racists, Vincent. But see— well, you know his dad was a cop, right?"

"Chris told me his dad was a sheriff's deputy."

She nodded. "There are a lot of crazy, heavily armed people up in the southern Appalachians. Since the meth started spreading, and the oxy, they've gotten crazier, more dangerous. Roy was shot at three times in five years. Then he was hit, badly wounded. But Roy survived and went back to work. Then…" She gave a dry chuckle. "…three years later—lung cancer. Bullets couldn't kill him—but cigarettes did!"

"Chris mentioned that…"

"After Roy died, Bobby kind of lost his way. He'd been talking about going to a police academy, becoming a deputy like his dad. Only he had some problems. Pot smoking, drinking, a DUI. Then he got into oxycontin. Claimed he was going to clean up his act. Then Roy died and Chris was killed… They died within a year of one another!"

21

Vince grimaced. "Hard to process all that. The white nationalists have been stepping up their online recruitment of young men—they look for guys who are kind of lost, and angry. Looking for someone to blame."

She gave him a vigorous nod. "That's just what happened! Anyway, I lost touch with him for five months while he was with that man Gustafson—that's their deep-pockets, their so-called visionary. Their little Hitler, really. Bobby said he was getting special training that would 'save America'. Then he came over here one day and…" She shrugged. "…he said he was done. Said they were planning something. That a lot of innocent people would die. He wanted no part of it. He packed a bag, got on his motorcycle, went to the base one last time. That's the last I heard of him."

"You tell the feds about this… attack?"

"I thought about it for a whole week. Finally decided I had to tell them. So I told the FBI. An agent drove all the way up to the house and talked to me. I didn't know any details. Just what I told you. He wanted me to keep it all quiet, said they were aware of the Brethren and would see what they could find out. That was months ago…"

Vince sipped a little of his whiskey and said, "The feds are more careful now. After the Waco thing."

"Apparently these domestic terrorist cells are always making some ugly plan and usually nothing comes of it. That's what Agent Chang said. So maybe the FBI's not taking it all that seriously. But meanwhile—where's Bobby?"

"Yeah. It's… You're probably on tenterhooks all the time."

"I am." She drank a little more, then put the glass on the floor. "I have to drive home; I'd better skip the rest of that drink. Vincent, what was it that Chris asked you to do for him?"

I'm going to have to tell her…

"When he was dying, I tied off his arm… and…" She didn't need to know all the details. How Chris had picked up the severed hand and clutched it to him. "As I guess you know, he came home… his body came home… missing a hand."

"Yes. I assumed it was lost or…"

"No. I wasn't sure how to tell you about this, so I didn't say anything. It was torn off in the explosion. He asked me to take the hand, preserve it, bring it here. Bury it under the porch of this cabin."

Her mouth dropped open. "What? *Really?*"

"Really. We wrapped it up well as we could, but then PASI took it, said they'd preserve it, get it to the family. They would not release it to me. Friend of mine in PASI said they never turned it over to anyone. It's taken me all this time to find out what happened to it. Just got hold of it about ten days ago. It was frozen. Their medic, a man named Charlie Ames, kept it in a freezer. It was kind of forgotten. Finally, he got in touch with me, and… it's a long story. But I have it now, preserved in alcohol. Right here with me."

She snapped to stare at his backpack. "My son's hand… *is in that backpack?*"

Vince winced. Maybe he should have done the burial entirely on the Q.T. But… it didn't seem right, her not knowing. This was her property. "Yes ma'am. It's there. It was the last thing he asked me to do. I couldn't… *not* do it. I thought I might get it done tonight. I didn't actually think you'd be here. I thought we'd probably meet at your house tomorrow…"

"You told me you'd get here this evening." She smiled wanly. "Didn't mean to ambush you."

"That's alright. I understand."

"Listen—I don't want to see his hand. You go ahead and pry up the boards out there. There are some tools in that shed out back. Dig a hole and put it down in there, in its plastic bag, and say what you want. I just… can't be here for that. But if that's what he wanted…"

"Yes ma'am. I'll take care of it."

"You don't have to yes-ma'am me, Vincent Bellator. There is something you can do for me, though. I don't know who else to ask. And it's kind of… a lot. Bobby said don't trust the local cops. He said at least one of them is in with the Brethren. And I never heard from the feds again. I was thinking maybe you could… I don't know…"

"Find out what's become of Bobby?" Vince nodded. "I was going to suggest I might do just that. I'll need to locate some Germanic Brethren away from their Fortress of Solitude or whatever the hell they call it. Maybe somewhere in town for a start…"

"Thank you for doing this, Vincent. Just see if you can get them to talk to you. I don't want you to get hurt."

"Getting hurt isn't part of my plan."

"Listen—there's some fishing tackle in the bedroom closet. Maybe for in the morning. And out behind the cabin, under a tarp, you'll find Chris's motorcycle. It's a Harley trail bike from the 1960s. Chris and Bobby rebuilt it together. Took 'em two years to get the parts. If it doesn't start, call me, and I'll pick you up. But Bobby was working on it a couple months ago and he can fix anything. I'll bet it starts." She stood up. "Now, I'll tell you where you might find some of the Germanic Brethren. There's a place called Tina's Bar and Grill…"

It took Vince about fifteen minutes to get enough boards off the porch, without doing too much damage. He got the folding

24

army surplus camp shovel from his backpack, along with the jar in bubble wrap, and brought them out to the porch. He set the jar carefully aside, lowered the porch lantern into the hole, stepped in after it, and got to work. "Maybe just a couple feet down, Chris," he said, as he dug. "I figure you want to be up high enough to protect the cabin." He dug for a while more and then said, "This cabin must've meant a lot to you. I guess you and Bobby and your folks were out here for fishing. Maybe felt more like home than the house in town."

Vince knew that a lot of people would think he sounded crazy, talking to the dead like this. They'd think his errand under the porch was crazy too. But they weren't professional soldiers. A lot of guys he knew talked to their dead buddies now and then. It seemed to help. And if there was anything you could do to honor a buddy who'd died, you did it.

He got two feet down, and then he tossed the shovel onto the porch, unwrapped the jar, and took one last look at Chris's hand, with its ragged bit of wrist, floating in medical preservation fluids. The fingers were formed into a fist; the skin now pale blue but otherwise well preserved. There was an Army Rangers ring on it.

"Chris, I'm doing this crazy shit you asked me to do, and I hope you're satisfied." He sighed. "I met your mom. Liked her a lot. I'm gonna do what I can to help her. Hey—she gave me the keys to that Harley you rebuilt. I'll try not to wreck it. And I'm going to make a promise. The guy who killed you… the head of the outfit that killed you… that guy Lopez? I heard a rumor he's working in Arizona now. I promise, my brother—I'm going to take him out."

Vince put the jar into the hole, covered it over, then patted down the little hump in the dirt. He said, "*Sua sponte*, man." The

Army Rangers motto. *Of their own accord.* "We took the trail of our own accord, brother. I was proud to walk it with you."

Then he climbed out and set to work replacing the boards.

Vince was up at dawn, prepping coffee on the camp stove, doing push-ups and sit-ups on the ground out front of the cabin while the coffee was perking, watching the sun turn the horizon from gray to rose-blue over the top of the forest.

He drank his coffee while he was getting the tackle organized, finding some fishing flies in a tackle box.

He carried the tackle box and headed west, stepping over Dead Springs Creek. It was so narrow it barely deserved to be called a creek; it was little more than a crooked moss-lined ditch streaming with shallow water. He kept going another half mile. When he reached Chickasaw Creek, he set off upstream till he found a wide, deeper place; a possible fishing hole. It was already jumping with trout.

Vince caught four of them over two hours, then carried them on a line back to the cabin. He cleaned them and fried them for breakfast in a dusting of cornmeal and pepper.

When he'd finished a third cup of coffee, Vince got the detailed area maps from his backpack and sat on the sofa to study them.

He found the place, east of the Talladega National Forest, where the gunfire had likely come from.

The headquarters of the Germanic Brethren.

He remembered the picture Chris had shown him of Bobby Destry. A slim young man with a brave smile and sad gray eyes. Was Bobby there, maybe held a prisoner?

Or—was he dead, and buried somewhere out in the woods?

CHAPTER THREE

A little past nine that evening, Vince showered, shaved, went to the back of the cabin, and started up the old Harley. It sputtered, then rumbled steadily. He smiled at the sound. His old man taught him to ride on a Harley, and he'd given Vince a '66 Bobcat for his seventeenth birthday. They'd gone for long rides out in the hills. Two men connecting deeply, just riding side by side on the road, never having to say a word.

Vince rode the Harley around the cabin to the road and to the little mountain town of Stonewall. Tina's Bar and Grill was right where Rose said it would be, set close to a trailer park and half hidden by a screen of pine trees.

He swung the trail bike into the bar's parking lot. A dozen pickups and SUVs, all of them with huge tires, were parked around the bar, nosed in as if they were feeding. It was dark, the trees and clouds cutting out most of the starlight. A single light-pole shed a sickly yellow glow over the parking lot and one small window with a Jack Daniels sign added a splash of neon blue and rusty red. He could barely make out the flaking old sign for the bar atop the square, flat little building.

Vince parked the Harley behind the bar. He noted a gravel road that passed from the lot to the trailer park. Someone was riding a dirt bike back thereon dirt tracks behind the trailers. He could hear its engine growling and whining, and he could see the single headlight strobing through the brush. Good to know there was a back way out of here for a bike.

Vince went around the corner of the bar and through the red metal door with its warning about serving minors. Inside, he was struck by the cigarette smoke first. He had grown used to Washington State, where smoking wasn't allowed in bars. The air was gray with it here.

The bar was mostly taken up by the broad backs of hefty men, with a few women peppered in. The men wore sleeveless t-shirts and football jerseys; the Dallas Cowboys and the Atlanta Falcons and the Crimson Tide. To Vince's left was an internet-based jukebox playing a Kid Rock song, something about "God knows why". Pool balls clacked under a cone of light on the other side of the bar. A tall blond woman with big arms and wide shoulders and a mass of curled hair was tending bar at the near end; at the other end an Asian-American kid was bussing. The smell of barbecued ribs was in the air.

Vince had a weakness for pool, and he gave the tables one longing glance before going to the bar. He found the only open spot. The big lady drifted over, light as a cloud. She wore lime green pants and vest, and a white, frilly blouse, open to display her tanned, sparkle-sprayed cleavage.

Louder than Kid Rock, she said, "What can I get you, little fella?"

Vince grinned. "Miller draft."

"You got it."

She brought him the beer and asked, "What's your name, hon?"

"Vince."

"I'm Tina. I hear a little Texas in your voice?"

"Ya'll ain't wrong."

She squinched up her lips in pretend disapproval. "We get trouble from Texas all the time! Well you're in Alabama now, so you behave. I wouldn't want to have to spank you."

Vince laughed. "I'll be good."

She winked and went to pour someone a Jack.

Vince sipped his beer, looking around as the music changed to Toby Keith. He spotted one of the Brethren almost immediately; the short blond guy, Shaun Adler, now in a black hoodie and jeans, looking sullenly into a tequila sunrise.

On his right was an older, more muscular guy with a blond flattop haircut. He was wearing a cut-off sleeveless shirt, showing his hard belly. He had a cigarette in one hand and an empty glass in front of him that he twirled between two fingers as he muttered something to Shaun. Probably his brother. The older one was sniffling, twitching, talking on and on in the frowning Shaun's ear.

Meth, Vince figured.

The tweaker brother suddenly slid off his stool and went almost at a run toward the men's room. Shaun closed his eyes and shook his head.

A heavy-set, bearded man in a cowboy hat came into the bar, looked around, and made a bee-line for Shaun. He was a foot taller than the short militiaman and probably outweighed him twice over. He was pop-eyed, and his bare arms were crawling with tattoos, so many they muddled one another. The big guy sidled up to Shaun and prodded him with a thick stubby finger.

Shaun twitched away from him. Cowboy Beard pressed closer, looming over Shaun, and shoved him into the bar, bending near him, snarling something. Shaun shook his head…

And Vince smiled to himself, thinking, *This is my chance.*

He walked over, stopped just a step away, in time to hear the bearded cowboy say, "Your brother is not going to pay me that money. So you got to do it."

"I haven't got it, Rendell!" Shaun said.

"He's snorted four hundred dollars of my goody-goods up his nose and if I don't get that money from him, I'll take it out of your hide, boy—"

Vince tapped Rendell on the shoulder. "Hey."

Rendell turned and jabbed a stubby finger at Vince. "Hey—back off, this here's a private conversation!"

Shaun gawped at Vince, his eyes wide. "Uhhh… *You?*"

Vince said, "Shaun Adler, here, is a personal friend of mine… Rendell."

Shaun seemed startled by that claim. Just then, as Vince went on, the song finished and another one wasn't slated to come on. The place went quiet except for a few people murmuring. Vince sensed everyone in the bar was looking their way.

Keeping his tone polite, he went on, "I have this feeling that you're *threatening* Shaun. If it weren't for the fact that the debt in question relates to a poison you've been selling his brother, I might just pay it off. But I can't give any money to a guy like you. So, I'm going to ask you to back off and leave the bar." Vince smiled. "If you would, Rendell—please."

Rendell was staring at him as if Vince had spoken in ancient Greek. Then he shook his head in amazement. He turned away, as if he were going to talk to Shaun—but Vince saw the hulking man's right-hand bunch into a fist, saw the tension in his right arm. The guy was going to try a sucker-punch.

If a hard punch from a man that size landed, it could do Vince some serious damage. But when it came, Vince was already ducking under it.

He jabbed his own right fist up hard into a cluster of nerves on the underside of the bearded cowboy's shoulder. Rendell yelped, his body swiveling past Vince with the momentum of his failed punch. Vince kicked his right boot into the hollow of Rendell's knee, making the meth dealer's leg buckle.

Rendell crashed down, his forehead catching a glancing blow from the edge of the bar, his hat flying off.

Vince took two steps back from the bar and waited for Rendell to get up. Shaking his head like a dog with fleas in his ears, Rendell got ponderously to his feet, then bared his teeth and reached into his coat with his left hand.

Gun, Vince thought—and as he formed the thought he spun on his left foot, kicked out with his right, cracking it into Rendell's right elbow as he drew the gun.

"Ahh, *shit!*" Rendell yowled as the gun went flying to clatter across the floor.

Vince got both feet on the ground—and Rendell lunged for him. Easily sidestepping the heavier man, Vince let the lunge go by, and Rendell ended flat on his belly, gasping for air.

The bar erupted into hoots of laughter and shouts of "Whoa, Rendell!" and "Watch where you're going, Rendell!"

Vince turned, moved a little closer to Rendell, and waited, letting the bearded cowboy get to his feet.

Vince set himself. Rendell cocked his left arm for a round-house punch—and Vince stepped in, exploded a Krav Maga straight-arm hammerfist, blur-fast, into Rendell's chin. Hard.

Rendell's head rocked back and he staggered, spun—and fell flat on his back. The wooden boards shivered with the impact.

Some in the crowd clapped at that. Evidently Rendell was not a popular guy.

Vince walked over to the .38 revolver on the floor. He picked it up and went to the bar. Men stepped quickly out of his way as he asked Tina, "Can I have a glass of water, please?"

She stared at him a moment, then nodded briskly and brought him a glass of water.

"Thanks." Vince took the glass in his left hand, carried it to Rendell and poured it on the drug dealer's face.

Rendell sputtered and flailed his arms, then looked wildly around. "Whuh? Where?"

"Rendell…" Vince pointed the gun at the dealer's face. "Sit up."

Staring at the gun, blood drooling from the corner of his mouth, Rendell sat up.

Keeping the gun trained on Rendell, Vince squatted down and said, in a whisper, "If you want another shot at me, go to the place Dead Springs Trail runs into Chickasaw Creek and look for me on the stream up north a little. Bring your friends. I'll be fishing there tomorrow morning. About eight."

Then Vince stood up and said, loud enough that the others could hear, "Get up, Rendell, get your hat, and get out of here." He lowered the gun. "Drive away. When I leave, I'll give your gun to Tina. She can do whatever she wants with it."

Rendell licked blood from his lips, then got laboriously to his feet. He opened his mouth to utter some face-saving threat, but Vince shook his head and pointed the gun at Rendell's face. "Save your breath. Get your hat and go."

Rendell's shoulders sagged. He hobbled past Vince, picked up his hat, and walked with all the dignity he could muster out of the bar.

The crowd started buzzing. Vince heard a woman say, "I called the sheriff, Tina."

Vince went to the window, squinted past the neon sign, and watched Rendell climb into a big white Ford pickup and drive off, its giant tires spinning gravel into the air.

Shaun stepped up beside Vince. "I guess I should thank you. He'd probably have busted me up." He glanced over at his brother who was coming out of the restroom, looking around in confusion.

"My pleasure." Vince took a pen and a little tablet of notepaper from his inside coat pocket. "I don't like drug dealers." He wrote a number down. "Here's my cell number. Call me, you want to talk. I might want to help you some more. You and your friends. Didn't feel good about having to rough you up—and bust up your weapons. I apologize for that." He handed Shaun the slip of paper and then walked over to the bar, pushing the revolver across it toward Tina.

"I thought I told you what'd happen if you got into trouble here," she said, shaking her head and chuckling.

"You'll have to catch me first," Vince said. It was his turn to wink. Then he put a ten-dollar bill on the counter, waved, and went hurriedly to the door.

He heard the police siren coming as he climbed on the Harley. He started it but switched off the headlight and rode it quickly down the gravel road, into the trailer park and onto the trails behind. He thought it wise to steer clear of the local cops, even when he was in the right. He could glimpse their flashing red and blue lights between the trees and trailers as they pulled into the bar's parking lot.

As soon as he was screened by the trees, he switched on the headlight and worked south along the dirt-bike trails. A quarter mile onward, he found a trail onto the highway.

Bobby Destry was trying to figure out how he'd come to be in this damp concrete cell.

Sure, the Brethren had dragged him in here. But he could almost hear his father's voice asking *How'd you get yourself in a position where they could do that, boy?*

He sat up on his bunk and ran his hands through his hair. He'd been here for weeks, and his hair was growing long. What time was it? He couldn't tell. There were no windows. There was just the twenty by fifteen-foot room, its toilet and sink, the bunk, a small air vent, eternally locked door with its little barred window and food chute, and a shelf of books. Most of them, including *The Coming Race War,* were by Gustafson himself. One of them had been part of the reason he'd tried to leave the Brethren. *The Protocols of the Elders of Zion.* He'd believed, at first, that the book was real—the plans of an ancient Jewish conspiracy against gentiles—until he'd done some research and found out that "The Protocols" was fabricated. It had actually been made up by anti-Semites to smear Jews.

When he found that out, he started wondering if the other claims the Brethren made were lies as well. The more he looked at sources outside their circle, the more he was sure the Brethren's sources were false or wild distortions.

But even then he'd been reluctant to leave. They'd helped him get clean from Oxy. He had a firm identity here in the militia. Something he'd never had before.

Then he found out the Brethren were planning an attack to kill hundreds of civilians.

No. He couldn't live with that.

He'd made the mistake of telling Mac Colls about his doubts and his plans to leave. Stupid, so stupid to tell Mac. He should have just left the barracks in the dead of night and never come back. He did leave for a while, then he came back to talk to his friend Shaun Adler, trying to get him to leave with him…

A knock at the bars. He glanced over and saw Professor Gustafson himself, smiling sadly at him through the little barred window. "You don't seem to be reading.""I read everything through, sir."

"I told you I wanted you to memorize the sixth chapter of my latest book and recite it back to me."

"I'm… working on it."

Gustafson shook his head. "I don't think you're serious about rehabilitating yourself, Bobby. I'd have to know beyond a shadow of a doubt that you are a believer before I let you out."

"I am, General! I *believe!*" He said it as convincingly as he was able. He had to try to believe—or pretend to. He couldn't stay here much longer without losing his mind. Going around and around in his head; pacing, exercising, talking to himself because there was no one else to talk to. "I *totally* believe, sir!"

"I am not convinced. And what are my options? It's not practical to keep you here indefinitely. I can execute you—which is probably the smart move—or I can release you. Which would be foolish. But… there *is* a test I could put you through."

Shaun swallowed. "What test, sir?"

"I just might give you a special assignment. With a chaperone, of course. You do it… I will give you a pardon."

"What kind of assignment?"

"Oh, well, as to that…" Gustafson chuckled. "You'll see. It's all part of the bigger plan… But you're also required to memorize that chapter I assigned. It's a short one. You can do it, Bobby. You have to."

"General—"

But then he was gone. Bobby could hear Gustafson's bootsteps receding down the hallway…

"Hold it!" Rendell croaked, stopping on the trail with one hand raised. His jaw was cracked, swollen, and it was hard to talk. In his left hand was the heavy Desert Eagle, the biggest handgun he had and one of the most powerful on the market.

The other three stopped on the trail behind him. Hever almost bumped into him. Behind Rendell, Glenn Hever, Tutty Tutwallager and Scarecrow Hudson were waiting, AK47s in their hands, mouths open, looking scared and stoned. Both the husky Tutty and the skinny, raggedly dressed Scarecrow had gotten high before coming. Rendell had told them not to.

The fucking Three Stooges. Why didn't he have better people?

"There's a tripwire," Rendell told them. His effort to whisper came out a rasp.

"Where?" asked Hever. He was a rail-thin man with a goatish beard and spiky, greasy black hair. "Oh—that fishing line in the brush?"

It was chilly out here in the woods in the early morning, and Hever's breath showed as he talked.

Rendell could smell it, too. "Yes, and keep your voice down! He told me where to come—and I'm pretty sure it's a trap. But I've been watching for shit like this fucking tripwire."

He glanced around him, peering through the shadowy underbrush for a sign of the big man who'd jumped him at the bar. All Rendell had been able to find out, calling around later that night, was that the man had given his name as Vince. Was this "Vince" watching, somewhere near? To Rendell's right was a slope crowded with pines and scrub grass. To his left the ground dropped sharply off, a steeper slope mostly covered by ivy and wild blackberry. About fifty feet below the trail, Chickasaw Creek wound through the bottom of the canyon, chuckling to itself as if amused by the four men.

Rendell looked back at the tripwire, bending over to see what it led to. Maybe a shotgun, set up to blast someone?

But then he saw what it was attached to. *Grass.* Just… grass, on both sides. Nothing else. That wouldn't have even tripped him up; the grass would've just torn. Why bother with it?

Unless—he was *meant* to see it. To stall him in this spot…

Then he gasped and said, "Flatten—"

But the gunshots interrupted him, two rounds, from upslope in the trees, and Hever yelled once—sounded like he was saying *"Yip!"*—as the bullets knocked him down the steep slope. He fell back, still clutching the AK, and slid down the slope, over the brush, flattening it down as he went…

And into a fresh grave.

Rendell stared, trying to be sure of what he was seeing. Yes. An open grave, perpendicular to the trail, hidden by bushes till now, had just swallowed up Hever's body.

"Holy fuck!" Tutty blurted.

Rendell turned spasmodically toward the direction the shots had come from, fired his Desert Eagle randomly upslope, the recoil from the heavy magnum round jerking his hand back. Then he ducked down, and the other two did the same, firing up the hill and then hunkering low.

The guy who'd killed Hever called mockingly down to them. "I really, *really* don't like drug dealers!" came a maddeningly familiar voice, from somewhere up in the brush.

Rendell tried to figure out exactly where the voice had come from, but it sounded a fair distance off and there was some echo out here in the canyon.

"I'm willing to let you go with that one casualty!" the man continued. "You have to throw your weapons down the hill, into the brush, and take off your shirts! Down to the skin, so I can see you're unarmed. Then you walk back the way you came and you *leave town!* You do not get to stay! If you don't leave or if you go to the cops, I'll watch and wait and I'll get you. One at a time. That's my only offer. You'd better take it, Rendell!"

Rendell shook his head. He'd had one humiliation at this Vince's hands already. He wasn't having another. Besides, he had a good understanding with Sheriff Woodbridge here. That was not something he'd find, not easily, somewhere else. No. This guy had to die. And it was still three against this one man.

"Rendell?" Scarecrow hissed. "Fuck this! Let's do what he said!"

"Nope," said Rendell. "You try to run, I'll shoot you myself."

"Rendell." Tutty whispering this time. "We can pretend to agree—then regroup. We've got more guns in your truck."

"No, you fool, he'll follow us. It's two miles to the road. We're gonna *tell* him okay, tell him we agree. You'll say that—I can't shout right now. Then we'll all three open fire up that slope. Maybe we'll get lucky. Then we move back along the trail to that fallen pine tree—you see it? We'll run behind it and then we'll split up and hunt him down."

"Rendell," Scarecrow whispered, his voice shaking, "I really think that—"

"Don't think, you're no good at it!" Rendell growled. "Tutty—tell him it's a deal. Then we open fire."

"Hey, dude!" Tutty yelled. "We're okay! We got a deal!"

"Now!" Rendell yelled. They jumped up and fired up toward the densest part of the vegetation, where this Vince was probably hiding. The guns cracked and rattled, tree branches spat splinters, pine cones fell, gun smoke thickened around them.

"Run!" Rendell yelled.

Vince smiled, hearing the gunshots cracking into the woods where he'd been before. He'd moved on from the "duck blind" he'd made in the brush, immediately after he'd given his ultimatum, running behind a series of granite outcroppings to the pine woods back down the trail. He figured the gang would go for the cover of the big fallen pine tree. If they went anywhere else, he'd still be able to see them head there from the outcropping he crouched behind now. He had a good view of the trail above the creek.

They did not disappoint him. As he crouched behind the rocks, he could see them running directly to the big fallen pine. They scuttled around the stump to hunker down behind the supine trunk. They were right there, in front of Vince, their backs to him, about forty-five feet away.

The clean-up was going to be such a pain in the ass. *Just get it done.*

Well, he wasn't going to just shoot them in the back. That was something he was willing to do when he had to, if it was a righteous target. He just didn't feel like he had to now.

He stood up, aimed the AR-15 carefully, then shouted, "I'm back here, idiots!"

They all spun around, Scarecrow even getting off a burst from his AK, the rounds cracking into the boulder that half concealed Vince. Tutty tried to run. Rendell was trying to aim.

He didn't have time for that. Vince squeezed off three semi-auto rounds, firing the rifle like a carbine, and the top of each man's head, starting with Rendell, just vanished in a welter of exploding blood, brains and bone.

None of the gang got off another shot. They slumped like puppets with their strings cut.

The echoes of the shots faded, and Vince listened for a reaction, from off in the woods. He'd scouted the area for a quarter mile in four directions and hadn't seen any campers or fishermen or rangers. But you couldn't be sure.

The only reaction to the gunshots came from blue jays, squawking in the branches, and a couple of crows flying away.

Vince had noticed Rendell's Desert Eagle. He'd make some calls and see if it was registered to Rendell. If the cops stopped him with it, he didn't want to be associated with a gun owned by a missing man.

Good chance it wasn't registered to the dealer. Kind of guy who'd want to keep his name off his murder weapons. That being the case, he could appropriate it. It was a good weapon to have. The AKs—*naw*. Bury them with the bodies.

Vince sighed. He wasn't looking forward to dragging the three men to their graves. He had more graves ready. He'd figured that Rendell might bring four men. He'd been close.

Burying them was the right thing to do. And you couldn't just leave bodies around in the woods. The sheriff's department would be alerted, at the least.

Vince shrugged, slung the rifle over his shoulder, and went to Rendell's body. He dug through Rendell's pockets, found his car keys, then took the heavy corpse by the ankles, and started dragging. The others he could transport one at a time with a fireman's carry.

"You're going to give me a back-ache, Rendell," he muttered. "I hope you feel bad about that."

Getting them all planted, covered over, the graves hidden, his footprints removed from the area—it took time to do it right.

He got it done, then he had to take Rendell's truck off into the woods, off-road it into a good hiding place.

It was early afternoon before Vince walked up to the cabin. He was hungry. He'd cook up some of the hamburger Rose had left him, along with some home fries.

His phone ran as he was stepping up onto the porch. Vince didn't recognize the number. He answered, "Yeah?"

"Vince? It's Shaun Adler. Um—look—I'm going out to… to see a friend, out near where we first met, in the woods. He wants me to tell you something and ask you something."

"What's his name?"

"His name… Professor Gustafson. He says you didn't need to protect me from Rendell, the Brethren would have done that."

The Brethren. Vince had to pretend he'd never heard of them. "And who's the Brethren?"

"Germanic Brethren. A… brotherhood. We have a special mission."

"Okay. Rendell would have stomped you before they even heard about it."

"I told the General that… He wanted me to tell you anyway. The other thing is—he wants to meet with you. He thinks you'd be a good candidate for the Brethren. But—no promises. He wants you to come with me to meet him out by our… our headquarters."

"Is this how you and your friends plan to pay me back for our encounter in the forest? You setting me up, Shaun?"

"No! But it's not safe for you in town. Rendell Saggett's got a gang. It's him and three other guys. They don't fight fair."

"Actually—they've left town. I had a little talk with him and he's chosen to leave. They all did."

There was a crackling silence as Shaun took this in. Finally he said, "Are you serious?"

"I'm serious," Vince said.

"Um—okay. But Vince—"

"Listen, if your professor wants to meet with me, it's going to be in public. Last night I spotted a roadhouse café—Pat's Eats?"

"Sure, everyone knows it."

"I'll be there tonight for dinner. Seven o'clock. I invite you and your friends for pie and coffee at seven-thirty. I'm not going to meet your Brethren anywhere else."

Vince hung up and went in to make his lunch. Maybe cut up some onions in the potatoes…

CHAPTER FOUR

Pat's Eats was a one-story log-cabin-style structure, built to attract passing tourists. The rounded timbers were painted dark brown, chinked with white concrete, and the floor was polished wood. The interior was decorated with old-timey artifacts, like mule harnesses and motheaten deer heads. The booths were wooden; cracks in their leather seats repaired with duct tape. Vince liked the smell, the redolence from decades of bacon and maple syrup and burgers.

He pushed aside the plate that had contained his venison steak and small salad. The pretty young black-haired waitress cleared it away. "Anything else?"

"I'm good. I'll just finish my Coca-Cola. Expecting some... friends."

She smiled at him, seemed to want to say something more, then hurried away with his plate. The little bell on the door tinkled and Vince glanced over to see Shaun Adler, Mac Colls and a stocky, middle-aged, wide-faced man in a neat, tailored blue suit. He wore a white shirt and a red tie. His gray hair was flat-topped.

His face, with its wide mouth and bulging eyes, was vaguely familiar to Vince. A newspaper report? Something about a professor who'd been forced out of a university under a cloud?

Vince nodded and gestured for them to sit down.

Gustafson sat across from him, close to the wall; Shaun on Vince's left, Mac Colls on Gustafson's right.

Gustafson gave him a wintry smile. "I'm Professor Gustafson. I take it you've met the other men?"

"I have," Vince said, nodding. "You gentleman like to order something? I had some apple pie. Not bad at all."

Maybe to keep from seeming conspicuous, they ordered coffee and apple pie. Three slices of pie and three cups of coffee arrived. Gustafson and Colls ate a few bites of theirs, and Shaun wolfed his down. "Totally rockin' pie," he said.

Gustafson was looking at Vince in a way that seemed analytic. A measuring; an assessing. Colls was looking at him with a kind of sullen vigilance. Shaun was studiously putting four spoonfuls of sugar in his coffee.

"I understand there's something you wanted to talk to me about," said Vince. "The guns I appropriated?"

"We found the broken ones," Gustafson said. "I assume you left them for us to find. Some kind of message?"

Vince shrugged. "If you like."

"What's the message, precisely?"

Vince smiled. "'Don't point guns at me'."

"I see. The other AR-15 is intact?"

"Yes. If we have an understanding, I'll give it to Shaun. He can take it back to you."

"What kind of understanding?"

"That you don't tell me where I can and can't go. I stay off private property. Apart from that…"

"You didn't have any right to be where you were," Colls said. "You were on—"

Gustafson raised a hand and Colls instantly shut up, as if someone hit a mute button.

"We're working at cross purposes here," Gustafson said. "It's a bad start. But I hope for a good outcome. You're a valuable man. You proved that on the trail. And you're a decorated professional soldier, Mr. Bellator. From a genuinely *ancient* family of soldiers, I understand. Your father. His father. And on… Martial ancestors going a long, long ways back."

"You *have* been busy," Vince said. He took a sip of his Coke. "How'd you do it? Fingerprints on the guns?"

Gustafson shook his head. He glanced around, probably confirming that the place was almost empty. No one was sitting close by. But he lowered his voice as he said, "We had a clear camera image of your face. There was that look at your ID. I ran it past an… a friend in government."

"Who would that be?"

"I'm not at liberty to say."

Vince nodded. That told him something. Someone fairly highly placed in national security.

Gustafson cleared his throat and folded his hands on the table. "You're clearly an intelligent man, Mr. Bellator. And you're an educated man—that's in your files. You know history and culture. You know that Germanic and Anglo-Saxon cultures created civilization. They created its art and science, its architecture, its engineering."

Vince wanted to find out what happened to Chris's brother, Bobby—meaning he had to gain the trust of these militia types.

Therefore, he didn't say *Actually, white Europeans got their number characters, much of their math and science and engineering from the Arabs and Spanish. And we borrowed a good deal of our chemistry from the Chinese—who had a developed civilization before Western Europe did. Then there was all the stuff we learned from the Egyptians. A great deal of western culture came from the Bible—the first part written by Jews, the second part written by Jewish Christians. Europe was a melting pot—Professor.*

Instead, Vince pursed his lips and nodded thoughtfully, as if he agreed with Gustafson.

Leaning closer, lowering his voice a little more, Gustafson said, "You *must* know that Western Civilization is under threat."

Vince thought, Yeah, it's under threat from guys like you.

He knew that "Germanic and Anglo-Saxon cultures created civilization" was code for "White People created everything good". It was white nationalist euphemism, employed when recruiting new people. They didn't get into the racial epithets, the outright Jew-hating, the eugenics and the Holocaust denialism right out in public. That would draw the wrong kind of attention.

Vince just nodded. And said, "Sure it's under threat. But what are you going to do about it?"

"We will create a new homeland for our own people, Vince," Gustafson said earnestly, now speaking in a whisper. "To do that we need to be strong, and willing to fight, if it comes to that. You'd be a great asset if you came on board. But the background I have on you, while detailed in some ways, gives me no clear sense of your philosophy, your political leanings…"

Vince frowned but said nothing. He had always voted as an independent. He didn't talk about politics online. He had worked too long in the covert world to commit that intel sin. The less people knew about you, the better.

"So first, Vince," Gustafson went on, "we have to know if we can trust you."

"And how do you figure on making that determination?"

"You'll have to come to our base, unarmed, and begin your re-education…"

"If you've got the guts," Colls put in.

Vince gave him a long, flat look. "Seem like I was short on guts, out there on the trail… Mac?"

Colls' hands tightened into fists on the table top.

Gustafson sighed. "Mac—do be quiet. I don't think this man's courage is an issue. Vince here is not stupid. He doesn't take foolish risks. He doesn't know if he can trust us."

"Very good, Professor," Vince said. "You're exactly right. I got on the wrong side of your people. Doesn't seem smart to let myself be surrounded by them."

"Of course. I give you my personal guarantee—my word!—that no one will try to… to ambush you. You won't be attacked. You'll be unarmed, but unrestrained."

"I keep my knife. Your men are packing major heat. I think they'll be safe. Just think of the knife as a—a good luck talisman. I'm never without it. It's on me now."

"Is it?" Gustafson frowned. "I didn't see it."

"It's under my coat. The knife comes with me."

Gustafson hesitated, and then nodded.

They shook hands on it. "We'll pick you up, right here, after breakfast tomorrow, if that's agreeable to you. Say 9:00 a.m."

"I'll be here."

Gustafson nodded once, briskly. "Let's go, men."

They all got out of the booth and headed toward the door, Colls casting a dark look over his shoulder.

Vince grinned at him, waggling his fingers in a jovial goodbye.

The waitress came over and said, "Another Coca-Cola?"

"Sure. You have wi-fi here?"

"Yep, we just got it a month ago. Boss thinks it's going to help business. It doesn't. The password is 'Eat at Pats'."

"Going to get my laptop from my saddlebag."

She looked at him impishly, trying to hold his gaze. "A saddlebag? You rode a horse here?"

"Sure. The kind with two wheels."

Next morning, as he was finishing his breakfast at Pat's, Vince opened his laptop and reread the pages he'd found about Gustafson. *Inheritor of wealth from his grandfather's tobacco plantations and father's lucrative investment in cigarette companies... Wrote his doctoral treatise on Nietzsche... Taught Germanic myth studies and third-level German language classes... Published a paper showing that German culture is heavily influenced by Norse mythology... His book* Concentration Camps Reconsidered *led to his dismissal from Florida State University... Was on the David Duke for President Committee... Attended meetings of Identity Evropa and chairs a white nationalist "Identitarian" group, the Germanic Brethren... Organized a group of people who unfurled banners over freeways, reading "It's Alright to Be White"... Investigated by the Bureau of Alcohol, Tobacco and Firearms for unregistered guns... Charges dropped, journalist suggests Judge was bribed... Journalist found dead, supposed plane crash.*

Vince looked at his watch. Almost nine. He put the cash on the table to pay for his meal and the tip, packed the laptop in its case, and took it out to the trail bike.

The autumn day was misty and cool, smelling of pines. He put the laptop in the saddlebag and straddled the bike just as two vehicles rolled into the parking lot. In the lead was a restored 1950s-era US Army Jeep, painted in green and brown cammie colors. Mac Colls was driving, with a big, wide-shouldered blond man sitting beside him. The man had a short blond beard on chunky face. Both men wore paramilitary uniforms, round green field caps and aviator sunglasses. Behind them came a glossy black Humvee. Shaun drove the Humvee, and the red-haired man at his side wore paramilitary uniforms and field caps. In the back was Gustafson, wearing a uniform. He had four stars on each shoulder.

Colls pulled up beside Vince and Gustafson said, "Fall in behind us."

Vince nodded and revved the bike. The jeep moved on, Vince steering the Harley around it. They drove out to the highway, the Humvee close behind Vince.

The short convoy drove four miles south on the tree-lined highway. Then the jeep slowed and turned east onto a gravel road. Vince and the Humvee followed.

After a quarter mile, they stopped at a white-painted steel gate. It slid slowly aside on a rail, and the jeep led Vince deeper into the dense forest.

Three miles on, the wending road took them to another white metal barrier, this one with a gatehouse. Two uniformed guards were standing to either side of the road, both carrying AR-15s.

The jeep pulled up at the checkpoint. Vince stopped the Harley and put a boot on the road. The Humvee stopped so close behind him he could feel the heat from the grill.

Probably stupid of me to come here like this, with armed men in front and behind me, Vince thought. Then he smiled.

One of the guards was a grizzled older man who had lost his left eye; the socket was blocked with scar tissue. Something about him said "retired Marine Corps" to Vince. A jarhead.

The other was a burly man with brown hair and fading blue tattoos covering his neck. He had a teardrop tattoo on his upper right cheek.

Ex-con, Vince thought. Probably schooled in the "Aryan Nation".

The older guy slung his AR-15 over one shoulder, stepped around the end of the gate and crossed to Vince. He patted him down.

"Knife, sir!" he called to Gustafson.

"I told him he could keep the knife, Gunny," Gustafson said, over his shoulder.

Gunny frowned and looked Vince in the face. His frown deepened.

Then he gave a faint shrug and returned to the gate, pressed a button on the back of a post.

The guards stepped out of the way as the gate rolled back, and the procession got underway once more.

Another half mile and the road emerged into cleared grassy land at the foot of a ridge. They drove slowly toward the gate of a fenced compound tucked against the slope of the ridge. There was razor wire atop the fence and men watching from a guard tower. Vince could see light flashing from binocular lenses up there.

A flagpole flew an American flag, and beneath it, snapping in the wind, a banner showed an Iron Cross. The gate slid aside for them.

Surrounded by armed men at the approach to a fenced compound, something clicked in Vince and he began to assess the area as possible combat terrain. At the top, the granite ridge rising over the compound was knobbed with two concrete emplacements. He assumed men were stationed in those emplacements, with weapons, watching the area. He could see a little light glinting off a rifle barrel.

About a quarter mile to the south, the ridge slanted down to a canyon, from which emerged a line of trees following a cut in the land that probably contained a creek or small river. Good place for a soldier to stay undercover, heading east or west.

The gate to the compound rolled aside, and the three vehicles drove slowly through.

They were now on a broad tarmac apron outside what looked like the entrance to a concrete bunker fitted snugly into the base of the ridge. To the right and left, within the high fences, were steel outbuildings.

Vince stopped the motorcycle, climbed off, and walked it over to the side of an outbuilding where it would be out of the way. In the distance he could hear gunfire echoing from somewhere west, in the woods. Automatic weapons rattled; carbines clipped out single-shots.

The other vehicles parked and Gustafson strolled over to him, looking pleased with himself. "Welcome to Wolf Base, Mr. Bellator. What do you think of our digs?"

"Impressive. Makes a man wonder, though—is this place supposed to keep people out or keep people in? Looks like a scaled-down penitentiary, Professor."

Gustafson grunted. "You'll come to appreciate it, if you stay. There's far more than you can see from here. This is really just the front door. The ridge you see before you is hollow, in large part. There are three levels of bunker complex inside it. You should call me General, by the way. The men expect it. And the women too."

"There are women here, General?"

"Certainly. We have no children on the premises, but eventually we hope to have a full, thriving community, spreading out around this organizational center. It's the beginning of a new nation."

Mac Colls and two other Brethren strode up, all of them looking very serious, as if on a mission. They had been ordered to keep a close eye on Vincent Bellator, he guessed. They all had guns holstered on their hips. 9mm Glocks.

"Where do we go from here?" Vince asked.

"Orientation," said Gustafson. "Starting with a short tour. Then—you'll get an education."

Coming through the metal door into the bunker on the ground floor, Vincent found himself standing in a kind of hallway bisecting an airshaft that rose between three other doors. Above, the shaft led up to the ducts and gratings of central air.

"First floor," said Gustafson, leading Vince and the three body-guards, "is comprised of barracks on the left, storage for food and medical goods on the right, armory at the back." The shiny steel armory door was set at the back of the airshaft, a little out of view of the front door.

"There are three levels in total, except for one small brig down below the first floor," Gustafson went on. "Stairs lead up to the other levels and to the emplacements overlooking the approaches."

Vince figured the entrances to the emplacements were the bunker system's weak point, since they were connected to the heart of the facility. Kill the men manning those upper gun bunkers and take a walk down the stairs…

He wondered what the emplacements were armed with. M60s? Tripod light machine guns? Sniper rifles?

"I'd be curious to see your armory," said Vince lightly.

"I'll bet you are," growled Colls.

"There are things here you won't learn about, and won't see," Gustafson said, "until you have earned our trust, Mr. Bellator. Would you object to my calling you Vincent?"

"No objection. How big is the barracks?"

"We have two of them, Vincent. Each one with sixty bunks. Only a fraction of them are currently taken up, but we have enough people in various places around the state and the nation to fill them all… and then some."

Gustafson led them through the door on the left, where Vince got a glimpse of a concrete-walled room arrayed in bunks and lockers. Two men in paramilitary uniforms sat at a green metal table with disassembled guns in front of them. They were cleaning the weapons and practicing assembly. Both snapped to their feet, saluting when Gustafson came through the door.

"General!" they both said at once.

"As you were," Gustafson said.

As a former professional American soldier, Vincent found this pseudo-military fakery both laughable and annoying. But he kept himself carefully stone-faced.

Gustafson led Vince and the bodyguards back to the metal stairs. Vince noticed another stairway, probably to the basement, farther down the hall.

They climbed the main stairs up to the second floor. "Lecture hall and video center on the left," Gustafson said, pointing. "Library and study to the right, conference room behind."

The third floor contained another barracks, across from a cafeteria and kitchen, and one larger room divided into administrative offices and a communications center—Vince got only a glimpse of a room full of computers, monitors, and a military-style tactical radio system. A thick-bodied man wearing headphones was sitting at a radio, muttering into a microphone. Two other men were working busily at desktops. Providing propaganda to white nationalist websites?

Gustafson took him into the kitchen next. It looked like the large professional kitchen of a university cafeteria. Three women in uniform were cooking; one stirring a pot at a big stove of shiny chrome and brushed steel, the other two doing food prep at a table. The room was pungent with the smell of cooking vegetables and beef.

"These ladies are from our Shield Maiden unit," Gustafson said proudly. "They're trained to fight, if necessary, but their main job is to support the troops. They're all skilled in nursing, cooking, office work."

The tall woman at the oven turned to glance their way. Looking about thirty-five, she was blond, though maybe not originally as her eyebrows were darker. She had a slender face, high cheekbones, blue eyes, a firm chin. No makeup.

"How's luncheon looking, Deirdre?" Gustafson asked, smiling at her.

"We're ahead of schedule, sir," she said, returning his smile.

She looked at Vince—and he saw a flicker of surprise in her eyes. Almost shock. But it was immediately suppressed. She nodded calmly to him.

He nodded back, and there was a curious sense of connection. Vincent sensed a razor-sharp intelligence behind those crystal-blue eyes. And he felt a kind of recognition for her, though he was sure they hadn't met before.

Vincent instinctively turned away, obscurely feeling he might be endangering her. He waved a hand in a way that took in the whole facility.

"Cruciform design, each level, General," Vincent said. "The floors laid out in a cross-shape. Coincidence?"

"Coincidence?" Colls frowned. "What's he mean?"

"I mean, with the Iron Cross flying out front…"

"*Not* a coincidence," Gustafson said, nodding approvingly. "The Iron Cross symbolizes the traditional German ideals of strength, faith, courage, and purity—all in a unity!"

"It's an amazing place," Vincent said, doing his best to sound admiring. "Is your thinking, here, survivalist?"

"If it comes to that," Gustafson said. "But in truth, it's a headquarters for the next stage of the United States of America. A stage of purification and greatness!" His eyes flashed with inner excitement. "A new world, Vincent! But it will come at a cost."

"This place had to have come at a *financial* cost," Vince observed dryly, looking around. "I'm guessing you paid for most of it. Your beliefs must be ironclad."

"They are," said Gustafson complacently.

"You said there's a brig. Anyone in it?" Vince tried to make the question sound as casual as he could. But he was thinking that if Bobby Destry were alive, that might be where he'd be.

"That is not a matter for you to concern yourself with," said

Gustafson coldly. "Now—let us go to the lecture room. You shall see some… home movies."

"General, I don't think we should be allowing this Bellator in here," said Mac Colls as he stood tensely in front of the desk in Gustafson's office. "Not even for a look around. I don't think we can trust him."

"That's what you thought about Gunny Hanson," said Gustafson as he stood behind the desk, pouring himself a coffee from a steel urn. "He turned out to be one of our best men. I wanted him for the same reason I wanted you and Bellator—military experience."

"We don't know what this Bellator believes in!" Colls protested.

"We'll find out. Trust me on that. I know how to put pressure on a man—till I can see him for who he is." Gustafson tapped a little Sweet and Low into the coffee. "Your real problem with him is simply, Sergeant, that he made a fool out of you. He outthought you and dismissed you on that trail as if you were nothing! I understand how that would be upsetting, Mac. But that's why I want him—because he's a cut above most men! Because he's fast and smart and careful. If Vincent Bellator is one of us, at heart, he can be the man to take the most critical job in Operation Firepower. We'll need a professional."

"I could have handled that job," Colls grumbled.

Gustafson cleared his throat. "Maybe, maybe not. But Bellator—I'm *certain* he could do it."

Colls shook his head. There was just something about Bellator that troubled him, and it wasn't really that the man had disarmed him. "It's the way he turned up here… the timing. He comes along only a month before we initiate Firepower. He's got an agenda, General! Suppose he reports on Wolf Base to everyone out there?"

"I'm not showing him everything. And you know, the FBI is well aware of this place. Have you forgotten that we escorted ATF agents through here?"

"We had to hide two-thirds of our hardware first…"

"And who gave us the chance to do that? Our special friends in government warned us. We are to an extent protected from the feds—*by* the feds! Of course, there are still people in the Justice Department who might like to infiltrate us—or even carry out a raid. They would, if we hadn't sold the ATF on the whole 'recreation for fans of the military lifestyle' business. The brochures really did the trick—I'm so glad I had them worked up."

Colls let a sound of exasperation escape him. "Sir, we can't trust *anyone* in government. How do you know your federal contacts aren't FBI operatives undercover?"

"Because they're old friends! I spent many a summer night with them at Bohemian Grove. One of them was my student, another was my teacher!"

"Suppose Bellator finds out about Firepower and tells some fed who's not your friend, General?"

Gustafson shrugged. "Bellator won't find out anything I don't want him to find out, I assure you. And—you know me, Mac. I let the gods whisper to me. I have a feeling this is the man who will change everything—I feel it in my heart. His coming here is destiny! *Das ist Schicksal!*"

"Is it? What if he's the wrong kind of destined man, sir? What if he's a mole of some kind?"

"Ah, well, if he turns out to be an enemy, then we'll kill him. I'll let you do it! If I give you the signal—you may personally shoot Vincent Bellator in the back of the head."

CHAPTER FIVE

Three hours, sitting in a chair.

Some of the toughest hours Vince Bellator had ever experienced. And he had undergone Ranger training, maybe the world's toughest. He had also been in "meat grinder combat", as they'd called it in Afghanistan. But this…

And yet all he had to do was sit there and watch videos without showing his real feelings.

He'd been trained for Delta Force to play a role if he were captured and interrogated. He'd been trained by the CIA to play a role working undercover in urban combat zones. He could control his features, his outward responses. He was very aware that two men were watching him.

But inside he was a turmoil of emotions as he watched racist videos telling lie after lie, falsifying history—he had a degree in actual history—and showing violent imagery suggesting that the United States would only survive if it was cleansed of "all non-white races except some few, kept at low levels, for domestic work".

His three best friends in the Rangers had been black, brown, and white. The officer he'd respected most was Chinese-American.

The best friend of his youth in Texas, Hector Gomez, had been killed by a white sheriff's deputy, rumored to be a Klansman, on a flimsy excuse. Vince had strong emotional feelings about racism. He was not down with it. He supported the First Amendment rights of racists, and that's as far as he would go.

Vincent Bellator tried not to hate or despise any group of people. But there were exceptions. He despised dealers in hard drugs like meth and crack and heroin and fentanyl, he despised terrorists of any kind, and he despised racists. The Germanic Brethren were racists and, in all probability, domestic terrorists planning a big move. Vince had heard that some domestic terrorists in the USA were raising money for their weapons by selling meth.

As he watched the videos, he kept his face wooden—except when he thought he should give a flicker of an approving smile. Sometimes he nodded, trying to give the impression he agreed with the utter bullshit propounded in the video.

But inside, Vince was seething.

Two uniformed Brethren had been sitting to either side of the screen, watching him the whole time he was watching the videos. He could almost feel their gazes on his face. The brawny guy on the left, introduced as Deek, had a close-shaven head that looked too small for his body. He had his mouth slightly open as he watched Vince, his eyes squinted. He carried a Glock niner on his hip.

The militiaman on the right was wiry, his face angular, his nose Roman, his big hands clutching nervously at one another in his lap. He had his teeth clenched as he stared at Vince. He carried what looked like a Colt .45 revolver on his hip. On his shoulder was a ranking patch showing two stripes. Apparently,

Gustafson had declared the guy a corporal. He'd been introduced as Corporal Marco Ambra.

When they'd met, Vince had asked, "You related to Antonio Ambra?"

Marco had smiled proudly. "He's my father!"

Vince had read about the guy while doing his research in Pat's. Antonio Ambra was a notorious Italian Neofascist, arrested for possession of stolen military explosives. There were numerous connections between American Neofascists and those in Europe and Russia. German and American neofascists were known to go to special training camps in Russia, probably run by Russian intelligence.

Corporal Marco Ambra. Overgrown, psychopathic, dangerous children playing army...

Vince wondered how far they carried this fake military stuff. Was there a boot camp? Was Wolf Base the boot camp? Probably something of the sort.

The last video finished in a welter of blood and martial music sampled from a scratchy 1940s German record, and then the screen went dark.

Vince managed not to say *Thank God that's over.*

Instead he nodded his head a few times, took a deep breath and stood up, stretching. "That was heavy," he said.

"Yes," said Marco. "It is."

"But what you think?" Deek man asked. "You ready to stand up and say no to what's happening in America?"

Yes, Vince thought. But not the way you mean.

"I've been ready for a long time," he said, nodding gravely. "They're taking away our culture. We have to stop them."

"Hell, they're taking away our *jobs!*" the big man said.

"That too. Any chance I could get a glass of water?"

Marco nodded. "Deek here will take you to the cafeteria. We will all have lunch. The General said he'd be there a few minutes late. I need to talk to him."

Talk to him? Report to him, more like. Tell him what Vince's reaction was.

They had lunch in the cafeteria, the women spooning the beef stew and creamed corn into aluminum mess trays. There were eighteen men present, and the three women brought pitchers of orange juice and milk to the tables, along with plates of bread and additional stew in big bowls. All three of the women were fairly attractive, and the men ogled them, but no one made a grab. Deirdre avoided Vince's eyes but he felt her watching him as he carried the tray to a long table.

Sitting on Vince's right, Marco told him the men had been out "on the range" and on the training field. They were boisterous as they talked and ate, with only occasional glances at Vince. No one said anything about militia plans. They'd been told not to, Vince figured.

When Gustafson came in, he said, "At ease, everyone." But the rowdiness dropped away and the men spoke quietly to one another as he took a seat on Vince's left. Colls, glowering at Vince, sat across from him.

"I understand the videos had some impact on you," Gustafson said.

"Yes, they did. It's... all stuff I suspected and didn't really know for sure."

"Have you given thought to becoming one of the Brethren?"

"Some. I need some time. Thought I'd go home and think it over." If he looked too eager to join, it'd be suspicious.

"Where's home?"

"I'm staying in a friend's cabin."

"You know, we are a militia, it's true, as per the Fourth Amendment, but we're also sort of 'Defense Department' for white nationalists. We are not the—what was it the Southern Poverty Law Center called us?" He looked at Mac Colls.

Colls snorted. "A 'domestic terrorist bomb waiting to explode', they said."

"When did they put this opinion out?" Vince asked.

"Just a week ago," said Gustafson. "We had the ATF in here a few months back, and they gave us a clean bill of health. But this kind of loose talk online may prompt some more federal harassment. I just want you to know that any actions we take are purely defensive. This country is being divided by the black slaves of the Jews—and it has been invaded by so-called immigrants. By communist organizers and the like…" He broke off, as if thinking better of what he was about to say. "Just know—we're a peaceful organization. But we stand ready to defend ourselves."

"You said something about my needing to—prove myself?"

"We'll talk about that another time." He ate a bite of stew, drank some juice, and added, "After we eat, I'm going to give you a short book to read about the Brethren. Something I wrote myself. Then I'm going to send you home to read it and think it over. You'll be given a special cellphone number to call for another meeting. Pass the salt, please…"

* * *

Bobby Destry was pacing in a pattern. It kept him from flipping out.

He would pace from the back-right corner to the front-left of the cell. Then he'd cross to the back-left. Then he'd pace to the front right. Then the back right. Then he'd do it all over again. When he got sick of it, he'd reverse the order. Then sometimes he'd make it more complicated. If he made a mistake, he'd have to do thirty pushups.

Pace to the front-left now. Then to the back-left. Then...

"Bobby!"

It was Shaun Adler's voice.

Two strides took Bobby to the door. "Shaun! You came!"

"Keep your voice down, man, I'm not here with permission. Take this..." He passed a pen and a notebook through the bars in the little window. "I heard you didn't even have pen and paper so..."

"Oh—thanks. That'll give me something to do. I'm going crazy in here." The words, long pent up in him, started coming out in a rush. "I keep trying to read Gustafson's books but they just don't seem to make any sense, the whole thing seems like it's just talking in the dark to nobody, man, like some guy on the corner—"

"Bobby, Christ, man, can it!" Shaun said, glancing nervously over his shoulder. "Keep your voice down and don't talk like that, not even fuckin' whispering!"

"Look, I'll do anything he wants if he'll let me out of here..."

"He said he was concerned you'd go to the FBI."

"Just because I wasn't sure I wanted to stay doesn't mean I'm a traitor to all my friends, dude!"

"They have to be careful. They've got a big move coming up…"

"I heard him say, once, something about 'Firepower'. But he never said what it was."

"He says it's, like, a need-to-know thing, and shit. We got a new guy he's high on now—this guy disarmed all three of us on the trail when we were asking questions. Barehanded, man! He's like a war hero or something. And he kicked Rendell Saggett's ass! Disarmed him and kicked him to the curb, man!"

"Whoa, *Rendell?* Good! Rendell is scum!"

"Well Rendell up and left town, and took his boys with him! This guy scared them into leaving!"

"One guy did that? Who is he?"

"Name's Vincent Bellator. Used to be in the Army Rangers. He's here, on the base, right now."

"*Vince Bellator?* The Rangers? Dude—that guy was my brother's best friend!"

Shaun stared. "Chris knew him?"

"Yeah! They were close! He was there when Chris died, man! Kind of a coincidence, him being… I mean, Chris would never have joined the Brethren and from what I heard, Vince didn't seem like…" He shook his head.

"Um…" Shaun's brow furrowed. "Listen, that's kinda weird. Maybe you shouldn't mention that to anyone. Maybe I…" He shook his head. "I don't know. It *is* a big fucking coincidence…"

"I wonder if…"

"What?"

Bobby opened his mouth to say *If he's here to get me out. If my mom sent him…* But some instinct told him to keep quiet. "I don't know, man. Can you put in a good word for me, with the General?"

"Like he listens to me? But…" There was the noise of a door opening. "Someone's coming. I'll try to… shit, I gotta go…"

"Shaun!"

Shaun rushed off, down the corridor.

Bobby walked slowly back to his cot and sat down. *Chris's best friend*. Here? At the base?

He felt a sudden, secret hope kindle inside him…

After being silently escorted from Gustafson's property, Vince rode the Harley to Stonewall and bought some ammo for the Desert Eagle.

He returned to his bike, shoved the ammo in the bike's bags, got into the saddle, and decided to call Chris's mother while he had a good cell signal.

She didn't answer, so Vince left a message on her voicemail. "It's Vince. I'm looking into that thing for you. Getting closer. It may take a while to get another message from me, but I'll let you know eventually."

He hung up—and turned to see a short, stocky, scowling, fortyish man in a sheriff's uniform walking down the sidewalk toward him. The sheriff stopped across from the motorcycle, tilted his wide-brimmed Smoky Bear hat back, and said, "Would you be the guy who got into a fight with Rendell Saggett at Tina's place?"

Vince considered denying it but he knew the sheriff probably had a pretty good description of him. "We got into it some, officer. I understand the man was a drug dealer. I heard him making threats to a friend of mine and it kind of blew up."

"Saggett seems to have vanished. You know where he went to?"

"Seems to be gone, the way I hear it. Left town. You miss him?"

"Don't get smart."

Vince had almost said *You miss the extra income?* But that wouldn't have been wise.

The cop stepped off the curb and put one hand out, the other on the butt of his gun. "Let's see some ID."

Vince shrugged and slowly took his wallet out. He handed over his driver's license as he read the name on the sheriff's shirt tag. *M. Woodbridge.*

The sheriff looked at the license, looked at Vince, then took out his cell phone. Vince waited patiently as Woodbridge called in his DL number.

A minute passed, with Vince glancing up the street to see if deputies were coming as back-up. But the only people on the street were a couple of guys coming out of a tavern and a gaggle of teenagers gossiping in front of a Dairy Queen.

Woodbridge handed Vince's license back. "Alright. Nothing on you. But that could change, you get in any more fights. You're lucky Tina didn't want you arrested. That your motorcycle?"

"It a loaner from Mrs. Destry. Chris Destry was a friend of mine."

"Oh? Army buddies?"

"That's right."

"Where you staying?"

"The Destry cabin, off Road Thirty-two."

"I know it. Don't cause a speck of trouble in Stonewall or I'll run you in. No more—you understand?"

"I do understand, Officer," Vince said, putting his license in his wallet.

Woodbridge stepped back onto the sidewalk as Vince started the bike. He backed it onto the street and rode away. Glancing in the small bike mirror, he caught a glimpse of the sheriff watching him go.

Vince rode out to the cabin. There, he sat on the porch and read as much as he could stand of the books that Gustafson had given him so that he could be reasonably conversant in Brethren rhetoric.

Two hours of soaking up lies, distortions, unsupported assertions, falsehoods about history, and near-psychotic rhetoric was all he could bear. Then he went about the wooded areas around the cabin, setting up old-fashioned warning lines: fishing lines attached to cans and sticks, whatever he could find that would make noise. It wasn't impossible that Gustafson would decide he was a liability...

He went fishing for a few hours, and that night he cleaned Rendell's Desert Eagle, read twenty pages of a volume of Abraham Lincoln's letters, which he'd brought in his pack, and went to bed.

He lay in his bed for a while, hands laced behind his head, thinking about the encounter with Sheriff Woodbridge. It had to happen. He gets in a very public fight with Rendell Saggett, said drug dealer suddenly departs town, leaving everything in his house. Isn't answering calls. Someone could have killed him. But then, the sheriff probably finds it hard to believe that one person killed all Rendell's men, too.

After the fight in Tina's, Vince's gut had told him that Rendell Saggett could be coming after him. So he'd set it up on his own terms. Then he waited to be sure the gang was there to kill him.

Now to Vince Bellator, that next step, outmaneuvering and killing the drug gang, was not only just and sensible. It was plain self-defense. But the law wouldn't see it that way.

Should he let it bother him? Killing three men and burying them in the woods…

Did it bother him, deep down?

He had to say—nope, it didn't bother him. Maybe it was all the extra-judicial killing he'd done for Delta Force. And in the Yucatan. You kind of lost your ability to let it worry you…

He had no trouble getting to sleep.

The next morning he went jogging, did a full regime of Ranger calisthenics, and went fishing again. Later, he forced himself to read more of Gustafson's book. When he couldn't stand that any more, he rode the Harley into town.

Drinking a beer at Pat's Eats after dinner, Vince opened his laptop and looked up the Southern Poverty Law Center article about the Germanic Brethren. The article assessed content from the Brethren's propaganda arm and concluded: *It would be easy to dismiss these NeoNazis as merely dilettantes, German-mythology fetishists, but their leader, Raoul Gustafson, styles himself as the commanding officer, the 'General' of a large group of armed men who wear quasi-military uniforms. He claims his Wolf Base is only a recreational center for gun and military enthusiasts. But the rhetoric speaks again and again of "revolutionary action" to restore pre-Civil War America. The Germanic Brethren are Neo-Confederates, anti-Semites, Klan-affiliated neo-Nazis—and armed with semi-automatic weapons, at least. They may well be a domestic terrorist bomb waiting to explode… They often use the white supremacist codename for "coming race war", which is "the Big Boogaloo" or just "the boogaloo"…*

Vince laughed softly to himself at that. "The 'boogaloo'."

I could walk away from this, Vince told himself. Best to just get Bobby out, if he can, and walk the hell away from these brainwashed idiots.

He said it to himself to hear what his conscience would say in reply. He sighed when it responded.

You know what you have to do, it told him. *You have the skills. Someone has to do it...*

He got out his phone and called the special number that Gustafson had given him. A man answered, and Vince said, "This is Vince Bellator. Tell the General that I'm ready to boogaloo."

Then he hung up, and began waiting.

CHAPTER SIX

Midmorning, late October, and Vince was standing in a light rain encircled by fifteen men as he picked up a three hundred-pound oak log in a deadlift. He finished the lift, then squatted, and did it again.

"He's got good form," said Marco approvingly. "Not that easy to have with those logs."

It was part of Wolf Base's "Centurion Method" fitness training, something Vince had been taking part in for two weeks.

They passed small boulders bucket brigade-style to one another; they ran with backpacks full of rocks; they lifted logs and tried to run upstream in shoulder-deep water. The whole thing was a fad amongst white-power militia groups. Because it had the Old Europe feel to it, Gustafson had taken to it wholeheartedly.

Two more lifts and Marco said, "That's enough, Vince. Who's next?"

"I got this," said the big blond with the carefully cropped beard. He'd been one of Vince's original escorts, that first day. He was pale as you can be without albinism; his eyebrows were blond and his eyes were gray-blue. He was wearing a paramilitary uniform, just as Vince and the other men were. Bjorn, his name was. He had a slight Norwegian accent.

Vince dropped the log, wiped sweat from his forehead with the back of his hand, and got into the circle with the others. He watched Bjorn make a point of doing two more deadlifts than he'd done.

He noted the three Shield Maidens coming through the meadow between the creek and the access road, bringing baskets of juice and protein bars down to the trainees. They wore their uniforms with short military jackets against the increasing chill.

Marco called a break. Eating a protein bar and drinking cranberry juice, Vince sidled up to Wynn Foster, who was sitting on the log Vince had dropped. Wynn wasn't a log lifter, Vince reflected; he was a log sitter. "Hey, Wynn. How's the training going?"

Vince hadn't left the base for two weeks. He'd been quietly asking around, trying to find out what the militia's big plan was—but he did it slowly, carefully, to evade suspicion. He'd made no headway. And Gustafson had told him nothing more.

"I'm keeping up," Wynn said through mouthfuls of protein bar. "Not my forte. I work in the comm center, usually."

"You're probably part of the coordination of all those guys out there in the country?"

"I guess. Yeah. I keep charge. Count heads. I do a lot of IT security too. Fucking deep-state hackers keep trying to break in…"

"All those Brethren across the country—must be hard to keep a lid on security. Some people are careless. When you've got, what, a thousand guys talking…"

"It's not a thousand. Two hundred and change. I mean—the fully committed ones. They know better than to talk."

"About the boogaloo? There's lots of talk about it."

"Not many know… the how and where."

So it's gone that far, Vince thought. There's a how and a where.

"The boogaloo is coming," Vince said, nodding, just as if he knew. "They have to know."

Wynn frowned. "The General told you?"

"He told me some things. It's still quite a ways off. I'm antsy. I want to get out there and kick some ass."

"It's not that long off." He stood up, kind of abruptly. "I'd better get back up there and check my… project."

Wondering if he'd pushed too hard, Vince watched him walking off.

"We're going on a trail run next," Marco announced. "Pile up your trash over here and line up. You know the drill…"

Two of the women were heading back up to the house, Vince noticed, but Deirdre was walking off into the woods, carrying a basket.

He got in line for the run, just behind Deek, which made Vince the last man on the run. Vince asked, "That blond really headed into the woods all by her lonesome?"

Deek was already watching her walk onto a game trail and into the brush. "The General, he's all into wild edible plants and mushrooms. Says women of the olden times would gather them. That Deirdre girl knows the right ones so she heads out there to pick 'em. Goes out there… all alone."

Marco blew a whistle and the run began. The trail run went in stages, the man in the lead taking thirty seconds to get out ahead, the next man going out thirty seconds after him. They weren't allowed to bunch up on the trail. Vince started out half a minute after Deek, running along the well-trod trail that wound up and down a series of low hills.

It was a three-mile route that looped back close to the starting point, and Vince was having to work at it to keep from gaining too much on the leadfooted Deek. They were almost back at the training field, a quarter mile away, when Vince saw Deek glance nervously around, then cut off the trail, into the forest.

He was taking a route through the brush that would intercept Deirdre.

Acting on instinct, Vince followed. He was quickly under cover of the black gum and kudzu-coated fallen logs and granite outcroppings rising from the uneven ground. He could follow Deek's trail easily; it was deeply marked in the dry leaves fallen from the stand of shagbark hickory.

Vince followed as quietly as he could. Ten minutes on, he came to a rise overlooking a narrow clearing. He could see Deirdre, hunkered down, using a satellite phone. In front of her was a trench with an aluminum box in it where she'd kept the satphone hidden. A grass sod covering was pushed to one side. Nearby was her basket of wild plants and mushrooms. But evidently that was only her excuse for coming out here alone. She was here to call someone, in private.

"Holy shit," Vince murmured. Deirdre was quite likely an undercover federal agent.

Deek burst out of the underbrush, a few yards north of her.

She gasped, dropped the phone and reached into the box—but Deek sprinted to her before she could bring the gun out and get it into play. He threw himself on her, pressing her onto her back, grabbing the wrist of her gun hand.

Vince leapt off the rise, landed heavily but stayed upright, and dashed toward the two. He was sorry he didn't have his knife. The Brethren didn't allow weapons during Centurion training. The combat blade was in the locker next to his bunk.

"All I wanted was some nookie, and come to find out you're a spy, bitch!" Deek cackled as he held her down. "Now you're gonna give me some and then I'm taking you back to the General!"

She struggled, tried to knee him, but only hit his hip. She'd lost her hold on the gun.

Then Deek heard Vince running up to them.

He turned to gape at Vince—and was drop-kicked in the face.

Deek yelped, and blood arched from his broken teeth and lips as he rolled back, half off Deirdre, losing his grip on her right hand. She bared her teeth and grabbed at the gun. Deek's right hand came up with a large rock from the ground—and Vince kicked him hard in the brisket.

Deek doubled up, wheezing, dropping the rock, and Deirdre twisted free. She scrambled to her feet—and then Deek sprang at Vince, tackling him low.

Vince went heavily over backwards, inwardly cursing himself for carelessness. He struck the ground with enough force to knock the wind from him. Gasping for air, he brought both fists together hard on the side of Deek's head. The militia thug yelled, blood spraying with the sound. Vince shoved him off.

Shaking his head as if to clear it, Deek got up and Vince rolled aside to avoid being kicked. Deek's boot flashed past and Vince grabbed it, wrenching to pull Deek off-balance. The big man fell heavily on his side.

Deirdre was aiming the 9mm Smith & Wesson at Deek.

"Don't fire that weapon," Vince snapped, getting to his feet. "They'll hear the shot."

Vince got to his feet as Deek got up and rushed him. Vince sidestepped, grabbing one of Deek's arms as he went by, using Deek's own momentum to twist it. Deek tried to turn, but Vincent stepped behind him and got his left arm around the man's neck, wrenching the man's right behind.

"You want him alive?" Vince said, struggling to increase his hold, the words coming out as grunts.

"I—I can't arrest him…" she said. "Not feasible."

"Let me go you traitorous fuck!" Deek roared, writhing to get free.

Vince made up his mind. They couldn't keep their cover with this asshole running around.

Vince set his feet—and Deek seemed to sense what was about to happen. He pushed his head, straining his neck muscles against all the power in Vince's left arm. Vince suddenly released Deek's head on one side and pushed it hard on the other so that the man's own force helped do the job.

And Deek's spine snapped.

The big man went limp in Vince's arms.

He stepped back and let the body fall. Panting, he looked down at the limp, staring dead man and asked, "You okay? He hurt you any?"

"Not to speak of," she said hoarsely, looking in shock at the dead man.

"You FBI? Or maybe… a state police detective?"

"Agent Deirdre Corlin. FBI." She shook her head and turned to Vince. "I know who you are. Vincent Bellator, codename Charon.

I was with Defense Intelligence when I first started and… I saw your file when you resigned from Delta Force."

"Yeah?" Vince was looking around for a place to put the body. "They had you on the committee deciding if I was going off my nut?"

"Pretty much. We concluded you just… had enough."

"You concluded right. There's a hollow under that outcropping over there. We could shove him in there, block it up… Unless you think you can get the agency to discreetly come and drag him out."

"Can't be done discreetly. So you're not actually joining these people?"

"Not for real." Vince bent down and took Deek by the ankles and started dragging the body toward the outcropping. "Trying to find some stuff out. Personal stuff. Only it's turning out to be not so personal. More like…"

"More like you're concerned about treasonous sons of bitches planning mass murder?"

"Something like that. Hey—know how to get into the armory at the base?"

"No, it's got a heavy-duty electronic lock. There's a passcode." She watched him dragging Deek. "You want me to take an ankle?"

"You can help me block him up in there. Rocks, whatever. You had to come out here to call your people?"

"The militia takes away your phone, out here, in case you haven't noticed."

"I did notice… Jesus, Deek, you're a heavy bastard…"

"Anyway, this comm system is more secure… or it was till that asshole followed me out here. And I've got weapons out here. Gustafson doesn't give them to 'Shield Maidens'."

Vince turned Deek's body ninety degrees, dropped its legs,

then knelt and rolled the corpse into the hollow under the granite outcropping. "Listen—you know a Bobby Destry?"

She handed him a couple of hefty rocks and nodded. "I met him. Seemed like a nice kid, for a Nazi."

"He decided he wasn't one—and then he vanished. Is he dead?" He set the rocks in place. He'd need more than a pile of rocks. He'd have to use bark, moss, whatever he could find…

"Last I heard, Bobby was in one of the cells in the basement under Wolf Base. He why you're here?"

"Partly. You going to tell your bosses about what happened out here?"

"I have to. You're not going to come off like a murderer, if that's what worries you. You had to do it to shut him up. But listen—I didn't actually tell you to kill him."

"I kind of thought you wanted me to."

"I kind of hoped you would. It would blow my cover if I arrested him."

"Anybody ever consider…" He went to get a particularly large rock. "…that if you just let these pricks know you're watching them, they're not going to make a terror move? You know—preventative policing." He shoved the big rock in place near Deek's boots.

"Sure, we know that." Deirdre handed him a couple more rocks. "But this organization is pretty good sized. It's spread widely. There are all kinds of aspects we don't know about. Things we need to know. And Gustafson might just take a warning as the cue to make his move… He's a fanatic."

"They're going to wonder where Deek here went," Vince observed.

"We'll have to come up with a story. If you're staying."

"I'm staying. I'll think of something to tell them. But you

should blow this popcorn stand, Agent Corlin—give up the embed completely before you're blown. They might start looking at you closer…"

"You know how long I've been on this? More than a year and a half!" She rubbed the wrist Deek had been squeezing.

"You've been at this base for that long?"

"No, I was undercover in the Brethren group in Illinois. Been here for more than a month. We got a tip from a local woman… Anyway, I've got one of these knuckleheads chattering to me a little now—I'm close to finding out what their Big Boogaloo move is. Something called Firepower."

"That's the big push?"

She nodded. "That's all I've got, the code name—except it'll happen in Washington D.C. But *what* exactly will happen… I don't know. You hear anything else?"

"No. But I read between the lines that Gustafson isn't thinking small… Okay, put those rocks down here, I'll do the rest of this. You'd better get that basket and head back before they notice you're late."

"I've got to finish my call. I'll make it quick. If you find out anything…"

"I'll find a way to tell you."

"I can't make the same promise."

"Yeah, I figured. Cops! What're you gonna do?"

"We could have a dead drop in case I want to give you a message—or you want to give me some info."

He thought it best she knew whatever he did. "There's a Slavic/English dictionary in the library covered with dust, off in a corner."

"Okay. If I want a meeting, I'll move it an inch out from the rest. I run the library so I can be there at, like, nine o'clock at night. It's usually deserted—these people aren't big studiers. You can leave the same signal. We could sit in the corner and pretend to be discussing a text…"

"You got it."

She hurried back to her satellite phone. Whistling an old Jimi Hendrix tune about a watchtower, Vince finished hiding the body.

The rain began soon after Vince returned to the base. A real gully washer. It was a piece of good luck, Vince reflected. It'd help wash away his tracks in the forest.

After supper, as Vince was heading to the showers, Marco called from the other end of the hall. "Bellator!"

"Yes, Corporal?" Vince noticed he had his pistol buckled on.

"The General wants to see you in his office."

"No time for a shower?"

"Nope."

Vince nodded. "Let's go."

Marco escorted him there. Vince found Gustafson sitting behind his desk. To his left was Gunny Hanson, the one-eyed crusty old anti-Semite and former Marine, who was training the remainder of his optical capacity fixedly on Vince. Hanson had an Uzi in his hands, pointed at the floor. To the right was Mac Colls, one hand on a holstered Glock.

Gustafson looked at Vince inquisitively; the others looked at him with open hostility.

"General," Vince said, saluting as per requirement. He assumed a parade-rest stance.

Gustafson nodded and leaned back in his chair, tapping his desktop absently as he looked at Vince. "We've got a team out in the western property, looking for Deek Fisk."

"Yeah, I saw him leave the trail. I figured he needed to pee or something. But…"

"But what?"

"He stopped in the trail and looked around, kinda with a disgusted look on his face, and said, 'Fuck this!' Then he dodged off into the brush."

"And?"

"And I finished my run, sir."

"You were the last runner, I believe?"

"Yes sir."

"Marco didn't see you come back in with the others."

"I was there, sir. Marco was talking to someone and I followed the others up to wash for lunch."

It was almost true. He'd gotten back in time to join the stragglers going back to Wolf Base.

Gustafson looked at Marco. "Could you have missed Bellator, when he finished the run?"

"It's possible, sir," Marco said.

"This is bullshit," growled Colls. "He's—"

Gustafson held up a hand for silence. "Vincent—you didn't see fit to report that Fisk left the trail?"

"After a long time in the military, General, it is not my practice to snitch. I figured he had been out here a little too long and was headed off to town to get a drink. He was going in the General direction of the highway. He could be in Stonewall."

"We have people asking in town," Gustafson said. "We'll see."

"Maybe it's time for some R and R time, in town, for these men," Vince said, shrugging. "Send five guys out a day for a while…"

"You don't get to make plans for this base," Colls said.

"Yes, leave that sort of planning to me," Gustafson said, nodding. "Did you see Deirdre Johansen out there, Vincent?"

"When I was on the trail? No sir. I saw her when she brought us some juice before the run."

"That was the last time you saw her?"

"Yes sir. Is she alright? She's not missing, too?"

"She's just fine." The General tapped his fingers some more and then said, "Okay, Vincent, hit the showers."

Vince saluted and left the room—thinking, suppose the team searching for Deek Fisk found the body? They'd realized that she was in the woods at the same time that Deek had vanished. Put that together with the dead man, the hidden body. The snapped neck…

He had been the last man here to see Deek Fisk. Maybe they'd work it out. Meaning he needed to get his knife, keep it on him, and think about how to make a move if they came to "take him into custody". Get the jump, bring the knife out, blade to the heart with one hand, take a gun with the other, open fire, head for the emplacements on the roof—burst out behind those guys, kill them, then head out along the ridge top…

A vague plan, and just one option.

But it seemed to him that Gustafson didn't want to believe Vincent Bellator was responsible for the disappearance of Deek Fisk. Gustafson seemed to prize Vince. He had some plan for him. A particular use…

Which was… what?

CHAPTER SEVEN

They were out on the rifle range. Vince was sitting on a hay bale, Shaun Adler standing beside him, watching him use some very small gun tools to adjust the sights on the M4A1 carbine Shaun was practicing with. It had stopped raining but the ground was wet, giving out low streamers of mist, and clouds churned overhead. Eight men were lined up to their left, taking pops at man-shaped paper targets set up on bales against a grassy hillside. Vince, the best shot on the base, had been asked to help out with instruction. He had mixed feelings about it. He was teaching men to shoot better—men who might well shoot at him sometime.

"Vince?"

"Yeah, Shaun?"

"You know Bobby Destry?" Shaun asked.

"Never met him but his brother showed me his picture. Heard some about him from his mom." He tightened a tiny screw on the rear sight. "You a friend of his?"

"Um…" Shaun glanced around to see who was listening. "Well—yeah. He's in the brig here."

"Yeah? What he do to end up there?"

Shaun sighed. "Depends how you look at it. He left; just wanted out. Wasn't sure about the mission. Couldn't commit."

"Which mission?"

"Well—war. Race war. Taking back what's ours."

"What was his hurry? That war coming soon?"

"Rumor says soon. But you know—just rumors."

Guns popped and banged and rattled up and down the line. Targets blew apart. And Vince thought, *Soon? Does Agent Corlin know?*

"So—what about Bobby Destry?"

"It's just that… he could've got away clean, but he came back here to try to talk me into going with him. He said they were lying to us, that the videos, the lectures—some of it was lies. Maybe more than some. I was thinking about going with him but, you know, I got nothing else going on in my life. I was having a lot of trouble till this place straightened my ass out. I don't want to end up like my brother, you know? And…" He licked his lips, and then spoke as if trying to convince himself. "…I'm sure of the mission. The Brethren mission. Right? And you—you're sure of the mission, or you wouldn't be here."

He looked at Vince as if wondering how sure he was.

Vince said nothing.

Shaun cleared his throat and said, "So, I'm glad I stayed. I mean, *you* know what's what."

Vince felt a sharp twinge, hearing that. He kind of liked Shaun Adler, and it didn't feel good to deceive him. Maybe there'd be a chance to help him, later on…

Shaun shook his head. "But… I feel bad about Bobby. He

83

should have a right to his own opinion, you know? America and the... the Second Amendment?"

"*First* Amendment. But yeah. He should have that right."

"Gustafson seems to think you're our new star around here, Vince. I was wondering if you could say a word to him—see if he'll think about letting Bobby go. I'm small potatoes, man, but *you...*"

"I haven't been here long. Not even half a potato yet."

"You're the most expert guy we've got. Rumor is he has something big planned for you."

"Something to do with Operation Firepower?"

"I don't know anything about that. But I guess Gustafson's going to make some big announcement at the *Erntefest.*"

"Which is—what?" He'd heard the term before somewhere...

"The harvest festival. Like in old Germany. The Brethren have it every year."

Then Vince remembered where he'd heard the term *Erntefest.* From *Aktion Erntefest*—the Nazi code name for the program to exterminate the Jews...

Vince had just finished the morning round of Centurion training, beneath a sullen gray sky threatening rain, when Mary Lou, the stocky, black-haired Shield Maiden came to get him. "The General would like to see you." She had a slight Serbian accent. She smiled at Vince, in a way that made her cheeks widen and her receding chin seem to vanish into a dimple. "Um—right away, if you please."

"Sure thing. Tell Marco, will you?"

He jogged up toward the open gate of the compound and in a few minutes was standing at parade rest in front of Gustafson's desk. Behind the seated "General" was a PC screen hanging on the wall.

"You asked to see me, General?"

"Yes, have a seat, Vincent."

Vince sat at the chair across from him. "Any word on Deek Fisk, sir?"

"No. We've put out a national alert for him, as we suspect he's simply deserted. It happens, now and then. Such men must be found and…" He shrugged. "Let's concentrate on the business at hand." Gustafson opened a laptop and tapped a key. A map-style layout of a group of streets and buildings, unlabeled, appeared on the big screen, in brown, white, green and blue. Gustafson took the laptop in his hands and turned to look at the map.

"Vincent—you were an officer, with a lot of combat experience, much of it in urban battlefields. I need your know-how, your experience—some advice, really. It's for a… writing project. I'm doing a book about tactics, you see. So a what-if situation."

All this sounded rather rehearsed to Vince, as if Gustafson had sketched it out in his mind ahead of time.

Inside a green circle was a rectangle, probably meant to represent a large building… There were few other details. A blue indicator might indicate a river running a little distance behind the building. Five streets ran orthogonally from off the map to meet the circles.

"This is a hypothetical battlefield situation?" Vince asked.

"Purely hypothetical. Now…" Gustafson tapped the laptop and an oblong of red appeared on the screen. "Here you see a substantial gathering, perhaps a thousand people, on a green in front of a large building." He used the laptop cursor to indicate the red blob and the big rectangle. "Now, looking at the terrain, what would be the most efficient way, short of a bombardment or truck bomb, to attack that gathering, with maximum effect in the shortest time?"

"I don't know what the ranges are, the distances between objects; I can't see most of the terrain. I don't know how many soldiers are involved. If you give me a clear picture of the whole scenario, sir, I can advise you."

"Hmph." Gustafson stared at the image for a moment, then shook his head. "I cannot... at this time..." He broke off and switched off the image entirely. "Perhaps when you've proven yourself. And in fact, that's the other matter I wanted to talk to you about. I believe the time has come..."

"Yes sir? For what?"

"I need you to kill some people for the Brethren. Certain people in a certain place. Then we'll know you are one of us."

Vince waited a beat, then another. Then he nodded. "I'll need to know who and where before I can get it done, General."

Gustafson told him.

Before returning to Centurion training, Vince went to the library and pulled the Slavic/English dictionary one inch out from the other books.

A little before nine that night, carrying pen and paper, Vince returned to the Wolf Base library, took out a volume of Goethe and brought it to a corner table. He waited, leafing through the book to look busy and to keep his mind occupied. But he was tired—lifting three hundred-pound logs will do that to you—and he was puzzled. How was he going to handle this?

The targets Gustafson had given him were supposedly treasonous former Brethren, who'd started their own white nationalist faction. Theoretically, the world would be better off without them. They were just more domestic terrorists waiting for their moment, waiting to figure out exactly who to massacre, and how.

But he only had Gustafson's word for that. There could be a hundred complications. They could have kids around them, for starters.

There was an option outside the box. He could make his move now. He could kill Gustafson, Mac Colls, all the key inside people here. He could release Bobby Destry, get into the armory, find the explosives, destroy their base—and the other Brethren probably wouldn't carry out the plan. They'd be leaderless…

But then, killing Bin Laden hadn't stopped Al Qaeda. And from what Vince inferred, Gustafson was modeling the Brethren on international terrorist groups. Which would mean he had many cells, spread around the country. They likely each had certain orders…

He read a bit of the Goethe translation from Faust:

"I see my discourse leaves you cold;
Children, do not take offense;
Remember that the Devil is old,
Grow old yourselves, and he'll make sense!"

Maybe I'm not quite old enough to understand the Devil, Vince thought ruefully. What was Gustafson really up to?

The layout of streets, that rectangular building…

"Mr. Bellator—can I join you?" It was Deirdre, carrying a book to the table, a shy expression on her face. Like a lonely librarian wanting polite male company.

"Please," he said, gesturing at the chair. He scribbled a quick note.

"I saw you had the Goethe out—I thought we could discuss it," she said, sitting down. "I'm trying to use it to improve my German…"

He shoved the note at her: *Any chance this room is bugged?*

She shook her head. She was librarian here, and a federal agent. She'd checked.

He spindled the paper up and shredded it to tiny pieces as he murmured, "Couple things. First is, Gustafson showed me some street plans… Said it was a hypothetical for a battle. Wanted some tactical advice, how to get in, do the most damage, and exfiltrate. I said I'd need more information. He didn't want to give it to me—though it was supposedly all just a thought experiment. I think it's their target. And I'm pretty sure it's the Lincoln Memorial."

Her eyes widened. "Oh God."

"He said something about a big gathering planned there."

She glanced at the door. So far no one had come anywhere near the library. "Something's coming up—the Black Caucus is planning some sort of pre-election presentation at the memorial. Lots of black senators, big shot endorsers. Public invited. And of course, the Brethren hate Abraham Lincoln…"

"Yeah. You'd better get a warning out."

"Any more details?"

"I did get the impression he was thinking about using troops. He wants to create something like a real army."

"That's a big order, getting enough people there. But he probably has a lot of decoy activity planned. Simultaneous attacks in other places. I get hints of that from Wynn Foster. What was the second thing?"

"I'm supposed to prove myself before he'll trust me and give me the lowdown on their big plan. And he wants me to do it by killing some people. Claims they're white nationalists—but they're some kind of hated rivals, who've been spreading dirt about him. Run by a guy named Dex Stirner up in a place called Cracker Barrell, Georgia."

"Stirner! The leader of the Ragnarins?"

"Yeah, he mentioned Ragnarins."

She closed her eyes for a long moment and said, "And you're supposed to kill him?"

"Yes. I mean, if he's what Gustafson claims, maybe—"

"He isn't! Not anymore. He's one of ours. He's… I shouldn't be telling you this."

"You just did."

"Yeah." She looked at him with a kind of bemused irritation. "I do not understand why I trust you so much. But I do."

"I stepped in when the asshole had you down."

"I'd have gotten out of that."

"You sure? He was a pretty big guy and he had the jump on you."

"Well—probably, anyhow. I meant to thank you for that."

"Not necessary. How come they picked a woman to worm into this outfit? I'm sure you know your job, but the Brethren are mostly male."

She gave a wry smile. "Because Gustafson's pretty much an incel. Contempt for women. Uses them sometimes but he doesn't take them seriously. He thinks they're no threat."

"He should meet some of the Kurdish women soldiers in Iraq. They'd kick ass on him and his men, easy."

"I met them myself. The photo in the file wasn't the first time I saw you. I was a heli pilot in Iraq."

"Which service?"

"Air Force. I flew you and two other Delta Force into South Syria for a night mission."

"Insert outside Al-Bukamal?"

"That's right."

"That was you! I knew the pilot was a woman, but under the goggles and helmet and comm gear…"

She nodded. "You couldn't see me but I saw you and the other two. You were with a black noncom and a white lieutenant."

"Yeah. Lonny Freeman and Chris Destry." He thought about Chris's hand buried under the cabin porch. "Chris was killed by cartel shitbirds in the Yucatan. He's the reason I'm here. Bobby's his brother." She took this in, and he asked, "So from there you went to…" He lowered his voice a little more. "Defense Intel?"

"Yeah, for two years. Finished my tour in a basement at the Pentagon. Listen." Deirdre lowered her voice a little more so he had to lean closer to hear her. "Dex Stirner is a Bureau asset. We turned him. He's giving us a lot of good information. You can't kill him. Could be that Gustafson wants to kill Stirner because he found out he's talking to the FBI about him."

"But I need Gustafson to trust me. Because just stopping one attack isn't going to keep them from carrying out mass murder, Deirdre. If he trusts me… I can find out what the Bureau needs to know."

Male voices in the hallway. Marco and Wynn walked by, not even glancing in the library. Deirdre opened her book, pretending to pore over it. Vince frowned over his Goethe. He and Agent Corlin were silent till they were sure the men were gone.

Then she said, "Stirner has been requesting a move to witness protection. He must know someone's planning to kill him…"

"There is one possibility," Vince whispered, leaning a little closer. "But I'll need some information…"

It was the night of *Erntefest*. Overhead, a waxing moon went from shine to dulled glow to shine again as clouds rushed past it. Vince was standing outside the compound, one of a row of men in paramilitary uniforms, each of them pointing a long silvery cop flashlight upward, shining beams of light at the sky in lieu of torches.

But real torches, their flames guttering in the late October wind, were emerging from the gate of the compound. They were carried by twenty-one Brethren who'd come that morning from across the Southeast to take part in the ritual. The men, all in uniform, paraded out through the gate and moved to the other side of the access road, so they stood across from Vince's row. A wooden dais was carried into place in the gate, whereupon the three Shield Maidens stepped up onto it. They wore Valkyrie-style costumes, with wings and Viking regalia. Backlit, they sang through wireless throat mics along to canned German music. The words were German. They looked quite solemn.

Deirdre could have been an actress, Vince thought.

A spotlight struck the flagpole as the American flag was drawn down, and another flag went up: the *Afrikaner Weerstandsbeweging*, a triskelion formed of three number sevens, black on a white circle;

a wheel of sevens around a central point. It wasn't a swastika but the triskelion had that gruesome panache.

Nazi assholes, Vince thought. But the expression on his face was reverent.

Gustafson took the dais next, reading in German from Nietzsche, then from Mein Kampf and from the lyrics to the Ring of the Nibelung. Vince had just enough German to work out the source material.

It seemed to go on and on.

Then Gustafson addressed them directly, his voice booming from the public address system. "Brethren! Shield Maidens! Heed me! Soon, the great movement will begin! The world will change—beginning with this nation! The way has been prepared! Our people are everywhere! It will only take a spark and spark will light a torch! Torch will light torch and the greatness of America will return! The White Man will rise once more to his rightful place! Power will arise from fire! And fire will bring us power! Do you heed me?"

"We heed you!" the men roared in response.

"Do you feel the fire in your bellies?"

"Yes!"

"Do you feel the power of the fire?

"Yes!"

"Will you take the torch when the call comes?"

"We will!"

"Now—we will feast! We will gather in the courtyard, where victuals are laid out for our late supper. Beer will flow like fellowship and fellowship like beer! Bring your torches, electrical and fiery, through the gate, and they will be collected. Let the feast begin!"

The celebrants cheered at that, and Vince marched with them through the gateway, where they handed in their flashlights and torches and headed for the tables set out to both sides.

Vince got a paper plate of food and mingled. He stood there, toying with his food and listening, close to the beer barrels, hoping someone in the know would get drunk enough to talk about Operation Firepower in his hearing. As he ate, he heard the Brethren mostly talking about how big their four by four trucks were and what football teams to bet on. Then Gustafson was there, laying his hand on Vince's arm.

He drew Vince aside. "Vincent—your mission takes place tonight."

"Yes sir?"

"Yes… In fact, I'm afraid we'll have to cut your celebration short. Mac and Gunny Hansen will escort you to the roof of this complex—all the way on the top of the ridge. There is something you haven't seen there. It's quite well hidden. A helipad!"

"Who's flying it, General?"

"Marco is a skilled heli pilot. He's already up there. Your weapons and the briefing material on your target await you in the helicopter. Mac will go along."

"I don't think I want anyone underfoot during the operation, sir."

"He'll remain on the heli. And now…"

Mac Colls and Gunny Hansen, both armed with Glocks, stepped grimly up to them.

"Let's go, Bellator," Mac said brusquely.

Glad he had his combat knife with him, Vince followed them into the bunker and up many flights of metal stairs to a steel door. Colls unlocked it and they went up another three flights to a steel ladder built into a concrete wall. It rose to an open trap door.

Colls called out, "Sergeant Colls coming up with two!"

"Come ahead!" called someone above.

Colls climbed the ladder, and Vince followed.

They emerged in an emplacement, a steel and concreted semi-cupola, overlooking the compound and the land beyond.

Turning to look east, through the open back of the emplacement, Vince could see the silhouette of a twin-turbine H225 rotorcraft. It was one big chopper…

"Get aboard, Bellator," Colls said.

The big helicopter's rotors hammered against the night sky as Vince gazed out the window at the moon-glimmed peaks of the southern Appalachian Mountains.

Vince was buckled into a seat on the forward port-side of the heli. Colls was just across the aisle from him. Marco was flying. Mac Colls glowered straight ahead.

No love there, Vince thought, amused. He'd like to see me fail in this mission. Or better yet—die.

Vince opened the briefing folder again, rechecking the map and "mission estimates".

Estimated adversaries: *four to six. Heavily armed. Uzis, assault rifles.*

Primary mission: *eliminate Dex Stirner.* A photo of Stirner was included. Secondary mission: *eliminate his men.*

Gustafson's got a lot of confidence in me, Vince thought ruefully.

Stirner was apparently in a farmhouse atop a hill just half a mile west of the Oostanaula River. There were no houses close by.

Vince's loadout wasn't bad. He had already inspected the FN-SCAR—light Special Operations Forces Combat Assault Rifle—with six clips in a belt. Gustafson, as a civilian, wasn't supposed to be able to have access to an FN-SCAR. Vince had used them extensively in Syria, Iraq, Afghanistan and Somalia. There was a 9mm Glock, fully loaded, with extra clip. He'd already put on the chest armor: JPCs; a Jumpable Plate Carrier vest. There was a set of shortwave-infrared night-vision goggles.

The rifle, however, had no suppressor, nor did the Glock. There was no infrared sighting on the FN-SCAR either.

The loadout was in an unzipped, padded nylon bag on the deck beside him. The bag was not something he would normally carry into combat. It would tear too easily.

He looked down at the bag again and said, "Mac—no sound suppressors? They're not that hard to get. Easier than the rifle."

Colls gave him a look of cold hostility and shrugged.

"That your idea, to leave off the suppressors?" Vince asked, in a genial tone—though loud enough to be heard over the rumbling engines.

But there was nothing genial about the question.

Colls scowled. "What are you saying?"

"I'm saying it looks like you'd like me to get spotted and KIA on this mission. Or pulled in by the Georgia cops."

"You don't question your gear," Colls growled. "And you don't question me. We have rank in the Brethren. We have chain of command. You're a newbie, a private and not even First Class."

Vince bit his tongue to keep from saying *You wouldn't know what good military order is if it bit you in the ass. Neither would "the General".*

He had the skinny from Deirdre about Mac Colls getting a dishonorable discharge from the Marines for white supremacy activity and other misdeeds. The guy was a blot on the escutcheon of the US Armed Forces.

But he only nodded and said, "Sure thing, Sarge." Vince looked at his watch. "We should be approaching infil."

"Twenty minutes," Colls said.

Vince removed his seat belt and reached down into the bag, drew out a black balaclava face mask. He pulled it over his head. He preferred face and hands blacking but they hadn't given him any. He pulled on the tight-fitting black gloves—he had no desire to leave fingerprints and his hands needed darkening. He hung the SWIR NVD goggles around his neck on a strap. His combat knife was in its steel sheath on his hip. He buckled on the ammo belt, with its clips and the two flashbangs, and then holstered the Glock. Then he picked up the rifle and slung it over a shoulder and went to stand by the door, one hand gripping a stanchion, boots braced.

He felt a certain comfort in the routine.

Marco reduced altitude till they were just over the treetops and switched off all the heli's lights. It was now flying illegally, unlit and in an unauthorized airspace. Since it was a civilian helicopter, there were big numbers painted on the fuselage. If they weren't false markings, then it was taking a chance to fly into a kill-space with those numbers. Someone could spot them and write them down if the moon was bright enough. If he'd been running the mission, he'd have blocked them off somehow—maybe stopped along the way to do it.

"Two minutes out from the LZ," Marco called.

The mission folder—which would shortly be destroyed—had designated a plowed-under tobacco field for the landing zone. It was a quarter mile from the farmhouse the field was associated with, screened by a windbreak, and it was almost half a mile from the target. He had a compass on his watch, but he didn't need to look at it. The plan was for the heli to wait on the field, engines and lights shut down. Zipped into a pants pocket, Vince had a burner cell phone he'd been given for the mission, in case the H225 had to take off and a Plan B was needed.

The deck tilted; the big twin engines changed their tone to something lower as the heli dropped. A gut-plunging feeling—and then a double thump, fore and aft.

Colls was up, hitting a switch, and the big steel door hummed aside.

"Hit the ground," Colls said. "Twenty degrees northwest, gravel road, straight up the hill. You've got four hours max. Make it less. Now get moving."

"Yeah, good luck to you too," Vince said. He jumped down, boots sinking a little in the turned soil. The engines shut off, whining down to silence, the rotors slowing, chuff-chuffing to a stop, as Vince took the FN-SCAR in his hands and started across the plowed field.

CHAPTER EIGHT

Vince didn't expect to use the rifle. It was mostly in the way, for a job like this. But it was easier to run with it in his hands.

If he had to fire the FN-SCAR or the Glock, the shot would give away the game. Which might be okay and might not. He still didn't know how many men were up there—they might hear a shot and rush him from all directions. Too bad Colls hadn't given him a chance to choose his own armament. He'd have asked for a crossbow.

He slogged out of the field, climbed over a barbed-wire fence—easy if you have climbed over a few hundred of them before—and moved up through an overgrown apple orchard. The trees were silhouettes now, barely lit in the filtered moonlight. The air had the spicy smell of decaying apples.

Vince passed through the orchard and reached a steeper part of the hill. He climbed, soon coming to thick brush, and angled right, stopping now and then to listen for voices or footfalls. He heard nothing but an owl hooting and the breeze rustling the trees.

Fifty yards more, and he came to the gravel road wending up the hill. He'd be too exposed on the road; he'd move alongside it in the brush. Flanking the road were stands of hornbeam and turkey oak, and the occasional pine, all crowded by scrubby beargrass, witch hazel and buckeye. The trees were still partially leaved but the ground was swathed in the first fall of southern autumn. There was just enough room in there to move and Vince plunged in, slipping as quietly as he could between the shrubs and trees, his eyes adjusting to the deeper darkness. A night bird called plaintively. The scents of pungent plants and, somewhere, a dead animal, were musty on the humid air. He trudged on up the hill, sometimes having to force his way between small trees. Starting to breathe hard, he lifted the balaclava from the lower part of his face to give him more air. To his right, the gravel road was a dark-blue slash between the shrubs.

When he thought he was two-thirds of the way up the hill, he stopped under a pine to catch his breath and listen. Nothing but the owl, the night bird, and something rustling lightly overhead. He glanced up and saw two eyes glowing golden-brown at him. Then the thing shifted, and he could make out the silhouette of a racoon climbing up the pine bole.

He waited another minute, listening, thinking about the FBI agents who were in the area and the parts of his plan Gustafson and Colls knew nothing about.

Sweat itched its way down his back. He heard no sound of alarm and no one coming.

Vince started out again, and in a few minutes saw the road was curving sharply to the left. The moon had slipped out of the clouds and he could see the blackened remains of the lightning-burnt oak at the curve.

The brief had said follow the road up to a lightning-blasted oak at a sharp left turn. Around the curve, the road would quickly reach the gated compound. At that point there would be security cameras.

He wasn't within the observation radius of the cameras now, but he would be when he got closer to the target. He would have to look for a blind spot. If he didn't find one, he'd have to rush past the cams and trust to luck—and probably simply shoot some white supremacist knuckleheads who thought they were more badass than they were.

Vince lowered the black balaclava to cover the rest of his face, then moved forward in a crouch till he got to the blasted oak. He laid the assault rifle across two knobby roots, in the shadows, where he could easily find it later. Then he slipped around the side of the oak within view of the gate to his right. It was a red-painted metal-pipe gate under a strong light. There was a small gatehouse; little more than a metal and glass box resembling an old-style phone booth. The guard sat in the gatehouse looking at his cellphone— a thin guy with his head pig-shaved, blurry, overlapping tattoos on his cheeks, his mouth slackly open. He wore a brown leather jacket with some kind of vintage military insignia on its shoulders.

Beyond the gate, at the crown of the hill, was a large barnlike house with a silo attached. It was one of those houses literally converted from a barn. Windows and a front door had been neatly built into the old, refurbished barn structure. Two floors of rooms had been added inside. The silo was now a sort of tower, with little windows going up its side. There was a light atop it, and lights in the windows, and one over the front porch. There were supposedly no women or children in the place, but Vince was making no assumptions about that. His uncertainty was another reason he didn't want to use his firearms unless he had to.

There was a camera on the light pole at the gate and another one visible above the front door. Just standard home security stuff. The side of the house nearest him was dark, deeply shadowed, the silo blocking the moon. He doubted there were cameras on that side, unless they had infrared. Not impossible.

An ordinary barbed-wire fence enclosed the property, running up to the gate on both sides. Vince slipped through the underbrush into the darker area near the fence, crouched by the bole of a pine, and put on his night-seeing goggles. The view sprang out in shades of green, gray, and black. He touched zoom and looked closely at that side of the house. No cameras. But when he looked left, he saw a sentry coming down the fence line about sixty strides away. He was a stocky guy with a pig-shaved round head. He was carrying an Uzi on a strap over his shoulder, his body language conveying boredom. He wore a sleeveless Levi jacket with vintage Nazi *SS* patches on its breast pockets.

Vince wasn't sure, yet, if he was going to have to kill the guy in the gatehouse. But the patrol sentry was in the way. He was going to have to die.

Deirdre's report on the place left Vince confident every man here was a domestic terrorist or would soon be. He had no concern about killing them. Of course, since it was all extra-judicial, he hadn't run that part of his plans by FBI Agent Corlin. Nor did she ask. She didn't want to know.

Vince took off the SWIR goggles, drew the combat knife, slipped back a little from the fence so that he was hidden by the tree trunk, and waited.

As a young soldier, Vince had sometimes seen a man he knew

he would have to kill and had let himself think about what kind of man the tango might be; about the guy's possible wife and family, about who had misled him to become the enemy. Vince would think about how this guy had been born, lived his life, and come all the way to that spot—just for Vince to kill him.

Unsettling thoughts. He'd eventually learned not to think them. Now, once he was sure his target would be a "good kill", he did the job with ruthless, methodical efficiency and put the kill behind him.

He was aware he might have lost touch with something in getting to that point. But he was… who he was.

The sentry got closer, humming tunelessly under his breath. Vince waited till he was past him, then he went over the barbed-wire fence in one smooth motion—knowing the sound would make the sentry turn around.

The man turned, frowning, probably expecting to see a possum.

Instead, the Neo-Nazi saw a knife flashing, two dark eyes in a black mask… as Vince brought the knife out in a *tantojutsu* side-slash, flashing it out tightly, arcing into the guy's throat—cutting through his larynx. The sentry couldn't even get a gurgle out. The target flailed as Vince jerked the knife free and instantly drove it back into the man's temples, the razor-sharp knife and Vince's practiced thrust punching through skull bones and into brain.

The sentry slumped, already dead when Vince pulled the knife free. Vince wiped the blade on the man's Nazi memorabilia, sheathed it, and—careful to avoid the gushing blood—rolled the body under the lowest strand of wire. He reached under, gave it an extra push so it started rolling down the slope into the brush. He put the goggles back on and looked around, half expecting to see another sentry. No one so far.

Vince moved through the shadows across the weedy lot to the side of the house.

He looked toward the guy in the gatehouse. Still staring at his phone.

Maybe being a dumbass will save your life, Nazi boy, Vince thought.

He turned toward the back of the house, moved to crouch under a curtained window, listened, heard unintelligible male voices. One of them laughed.

Still crouching, Vince moved on to the back corner of the house. He listened, then looked—and saw no one. He slipped up to the back door, drew the Glock, and quietly tried the knob. The door was unlocked.

He opened the door a crack and looked through onto a well-lit hallway with polished oak walls. The corridor led to a door into a room where a brawny man in a t-shirt stood with his back turned, his hands in his pockets, talking to someone Vince couldn't see. On the back of the t-shirt were the words *White Lives Matter*. A swastika was tattooed—clumsy blue jailhouse tattooing—around the man's right forearm.

"Yeah I don't know, if they are going to bitch about us on the Whitesite, then we got to stand up for Ragnar and call 'em out for it," said the big man down the hall. "Anyway, I gotta go up and talk to Dex…"

So Dex Stirner is upstairs, Vince thought.

To Vince's left were a landing and a stairway to the second floor. He slipped through the door, closed it quietly, and stepped close to the stairwell, around the corner from the corridor.

He heard the big t-shirted man's approaching footsteps and

moved quietly two steps up the stairs, drew his knife and flattened against the wall. But his boots made the floorboards squeak, and the man called out, "Boss, that you?"

The guy stalked up to the stairs—as Vince swung the knife underhand so that it came up and caught the big man in the throat, cutting through his larynx. The big guy—square-jawed, flattop hair—clutched at Vince's hands.

Vince yanked the knife loose and within a tenth of a second had buried it in the big guy's left eye, all the way to the hilt, so that the blade was deep in his brain.

White Lives Matter guy went down. Vince cleaned the knife on him, thinking, So far so good. He turned to climb the stairs—and saw a bald, heavy-set older man on the landing above, glaring down at him.

He was wearing a flak jacket, swinging a Smith & Wesson .44 toward Vince's center-mass. Dex Stirner.

The feds hadn't gotten the message through.

Vince hissed, "I'm with the Bureau!"

Not exactly true, but close enough.

Stirner hesitated. "What?" He had a deeply lined face, and his teeth were bared and his forehead sweaty as he stared down at Vince.

Vince used the only Bureau name Deirdre had mentioned. "Agent Chang sent me. You're leaving with me!"

"Boss!" someone called from the downstairs hall. "What's going on?"

"Code?" Stirner grated.

"Wind of freedom!" Vince whispered.

Stirner lowered the gun. "You'll have to kill the others."

Vince nodded, hearing footsteps hurrying around the corner below. He sheathed his knife and drew his gun—two quick motions with his right hand.

He turned around and fired point-blank in the face of a scarred, blond Neo-Nazi. The man had an Uzi in his hand and he squeezed the trigger convulsively—but it wasn't pointed at a target yet and the burst crack-crack-cracked into the wooden wall to Vince's left, spitting oak splinters.

The militiaman staggered one step back, then fell, already dead. He slid down against the corridor wall to a sitting position, staring at Vince's boots in death. His mouth was replaced by a gaping wound. Gun smoke choked the stairwell.

Vince turned back to Stirner. "They were supposed to warn you."

"I haven't been able to monitor the… never mind, shit, here comes Tiso!"

Another rush of bootsteps in the hall downstairs. This wouldn't be so easy—the guy was warned, now.

"Tell him you've killed an intruder," Vince whispered. "Then back up—real quiet."

"Tiso! Some motherfucker broke in!" Stirner yelled, backing up away from the stairs. "I killed him but he got Conklin!"

"What the fuck!" Tiso called.

"Get up here!"

Vince went up the stairs, taking three at a time, and stepped out of view in the upstairs hall.

"Dex!" the man called as he pounded up the stairs. "Jesus, fuck, there's two of them dead! Who the—"

He got to the top step, turned, and Vince shot the Neo-Nazi

through the forehead before even getting a clear look at him. He went to his knees… and sagged over against the wall of the stairwell.

Vince turned to see Stirner poking his head through an open upstairs bedroom door to see who had shot who. He nodded to himself and stepped into the hallway, a small suitcase in his hand.

"How many others here?" Vince asked.

"Sentry outside—"

"Dead now."

"That's all except Trevor at the gate." He paused, licked his lips and asked, "Listen—did you kill the gate guard?"

"No, he wasn't paying any attention. No need to."

"For once I'm glad the kid's a dope. That's my son."

"You taking him into witness protection?"

Stirner sighed, then nodded. "Got to. I'll find him outside. Let's go."

Vince pointed the Glock at Stirner.

Dex Stirner's eyes got wide. "What? Why are you…"

"First—drop your gun."

Stirner hesitated, then reached into his coat and took out the Smith & Wesson, tossed it on the floor. Vince stepped back, giving Stirner enough room to sidle by. "Go on. Don't want you behind me."

Stirner edged by and Vince followed him down the stairs. They took turns stepping over Tiso.

"Where are they meeting us?" Stirner asked, stepping over the dead men in the hall.

The guy's not real sentimental about his followers, Vince thought.

They went out the back door, and Vince said, "The highway."

"What? There's no direct road to it from here—"

"We're going through the brush. Get going. Down the hill, west."

"There's a barbed-wire fence in the way!"

"Then climb over it."

"Dad?" It was a young man's voice, from the front gate. He was around the corner of the house from them. "That you? I heard gunshots!"

"Forget it!" Stirner called. "Just get over here, Trevor!"

The young man trotted into view, his slack mouth getting slacker when he saw Vince. "Who's that? What's going on?"

"We're getting out of here. We're going into witness protection."

"What!"

"That's right. Unless you want to be on your own. Make up your mind right now."

"But—this guy's a cop?"

"Never mind that. You coming or not?"

"Yeah, whatever..." Trevor said, shaking his head.

Vince pointed his gun at Trevor. "You got a gun there. Drop it. Then you go with your dad."

"Um..."

"Do it, Trevor!" Stirner barked.

Trevor shrugged and tossed his pistol on the ground.

Stirner went to the fence behind the house, tossed his bag over. Trevor stared in surprise—then looked at Vince's gun and followed his father.

Vince holstered his gun. "Help your dad over the fence, kid."

"Why we going this way?"

"Going to the highway down that side of the hill. Just do it."

Trevor helped Stirner climb over. The old Neo-Nazi cut his hand, cussing to himself as he picked up his bag.

Trevor climbed awkwardly over, then Vince came quickly after and pointed. "That way."

They followed a slender game trail a quarter mile down the hill, opposite from the slope Vince had climbed. They passed through a couple of fields of high grass and then reached the highway.

Vince was relieved to see the black Crown Vic parked on the road shoulder, right where it should be. The lights came on, went off, and came on again, as per the signal.

"That the feds?" Stirner asked.

"Who else?" Vince said.

"Oh Jesus, Dad!" Trevor burst out.

"Just do what I tell you, boy. We're getting in that car." He turned to Vince. "You going to tell me who you are? You don't seem like FBI to me."

"I'm not. But that Crown Vic is FBI. That's all you need to know. Get in the car."

Vince watched as Stirner and his son strode the thirty yards to the car. The back door opened for them and they got in. The Crown Vic drove away.

The feds would be at the site within minutes, and one of the bodies left in the farmhouse would be "identified" as Dex Stirner. The word would go out that Stirner was dead...

Vince went back up the hill the way he'd come, skirting Stirner's property, and retrieved the assault rifle. He started down the road, jogging back down the other side of the hill.

It was quick this time, and he was soon on the edge of the plowed field—where he saw that the helicopter was lifting off without him.

He ran toward it, waving—and saw Mac Colls standing in the open hatch, holding onto a stanchion, a Glock in one hand… and taking aim.

Vince threw himself to one side, and a bullet kicked up the dirt where he'd been standing. Then the heli's door closed.

The H225 flew off to the south.

And as Vince got to his feet, he could hear police sirens coming his way.

"Son of a *bitch,*" he said.

CHAPTER NINE

Vince Bellator ran through the night.

He ran across fields and someone's back yard and across two gravel roads as police cars raced up the highway in the distance.

He'd seen a Justice Department UH-60 tactical-transport helicopter coming down on the hilltop where the Ragnarin HQ was. The FBI would stop those cops from taking over the farmhouse. But Vince knew he was fair game for any local cop who'd gotten a call about gunshots up at the Stirner property—or maybe had gotten a tip from Mac Colls.

That prick.

He'd tried using the burner phone. No answer. Colls wasn't picking up, which was no surprise at this point. He'd tried calling Wolf Base itself—no answer there either. Had Colls told someone not to answer if the call came from the burner number?

Vince got to a highway and saw a police car's flashers coming. Conscious that he was still wearing a black mask and carrying an assault rifle, he threw himself flat in a grassy ditch by the road shoulder.

Had they seen him?

Sirens shrieking, the patrol car roared by and kept going.

Vince got to his feet, picked up the rifle. He had thought about burying the rifle and the other gear, maybe in a windbreak. But there was other people's blood on them—and his own sweat had gotten onto the weapons. He had no wish to be tied in to the killings with DNA. Supposedly the FBI was going to cover for him. But Agent Deirdre Corlin was not the head of the Bureau. A lot could go sideways…

He took a deep breath and ran across the road into another field. It was a slog across that muddy, cow-pat strewn field, and his balaclava was soaked with sweat. He tore it from his face as he reached the screen of trees by the river.

He pushed through the brush and found himself on the banks of the Oostanaula River. It was a fairly broad, dark-green river, snaking through the night.

Vince stepped up to the edge of the riverbank and threw the assault rifle as far out as it would go, into the water. Then he followed it with the mask, his combat belt, the Glock and ammo, his gloves, the night vision goggles, and finally the armored vest.

He kept his knife. He'd had it a long, long time.

Vince reckoned to follow the trail along the river to the next town—the map had put it a mile away—and dodge the cops while he looked for some transport. Probably would take two or three Greyhound buses to get back to Stonewall, Alabama.

"I've got a mission for you, Bobby," said the General.

"Yes sir!" said Bobby Destry, without a clue what he was saying yes to.

He was just giddy to be out of his cell, standing in front of

Professor Gustafson's desk, poised there in parade rest like a person who knew what the hell he was doing.

Mac Colls was standing behind the General with his arms crossed, watching Bobby narrowly. Behind Bobby was Marco, who'd brought Bobby here under armed guard.

It was early in the morning, and Gustafson was drinking his second cup of coffee. "Like some coffee, Bobby?"

"Me? I…" He would. But he didn't feel like he should. "I'm good, General."

"Alright, now—here's the thing. I'm going to need you to go on a kind of undercover mission. We have a big tactical action coming up, and I'm going to need decoys to keep them looking the wrong way. You're going to pretend to be wearing an explosive vest. It'll look like one, but it won't be one. You'll call the police from downtown D.C., and you'll say that some Antifa types put it on you, and they're going to detonate it. They'll organize a bomb squad and a whole host of people will surround you. Eventually they'll figure out it's not real and you'll act as if you were deceived. They'll let you go. But by then we'll have gotten our men into place for… our critical action. You can rejoin us after that. This is an important job, Bobby… can I count on you?"

"I…" Bobby's heart was pounding. "Do I have to go back to my cell, Professor? Until the… the decoy action?"

"Bobby—I'm afraid so. You were talking treason around here."

"I think I was misunderstood, sir."

"Mac here heard what you said."

"I didn't misunderstand a goddamn thing," Mac growled.

Bobby cleared his throat. "Sure, Sarge, but still—"

"It won't be long, now, Bobby," Gustafson said. "I'll tell you what—we'll bring you out for certain activities. Centurion training, that sort of thing. We'll have a guard watching you. You won't be able to talk during that time, however. A rule of silence."

"That's…" Bobby was aswirl with conflicting feelings. There was elation, to have some relief from the cell, and a way out of it completely, in time. And there was fear.

Suppose the explosive vest was real? Or suppose the cops simply shot him?

No. The Brethren didn't use tactics like suicide vests. That was Al-Qaeda terrorist stuff. They just wouldn't do that…

Which meant he could let the cops figure out there were no explosives on him. Then he could go free—and he could stay far, far away from the Brethren after that. He'd never rejoin them, not for real.

He saluted and said, "Yes, sir, General. Anything you need me to do."

Gustafson nodded, stood up, and shook Bobby's hand. "Good man! Marco, escort this man to the cafeteria, give him some food, then take him back to his cell."

"Yes sir! Come on, Destry."

Gustafson watched as Marco escorted Bobby Destry from the room. Then he nodded to himself. "He will be useful."

Mac turned to Gustafson and said, "Suppose he figures out the explosives are real?"

"He won't. He has no expertise of that kind." He put some artificial sugar in his coffee and added, "When we detonate the vest, he will die so quickly he won't even feel it. A good death, in a great cause."

"The word has come that Dex Stirner was found shot to death, sir," Mac said.

"Ah! So it was confirmed! Wonderful! But what about Bellator?"

"As to that, General—no word." With a private smile, Mac added, "I suspect the police picked him up."

"That would be a shame. I had plans for him. And suppose he tells the police who ordered the assassination of Stirner?"

"The local sheriff's department, over there, is run by Jake Ferret, General."

"Oh—I'd forgotten! Jake's one of us! So if Bellator looks like he's going to flip on us…"

"Yes sir. Jake will find a good reason the prisoner had to be shot. Trying to escape, I imagine…"

Vince had slept most of the way on the two buses, catnapping at times, other times sinking into the deep sleep of exhaustion.

He was asleep now, dreaming that Chris Destry was asking if he could have his hand back…

"Stonewall, Alabama, folks," said a man shouting from a Black Hawk helicopter.

The helicopter fired a rocket right at Vince…

And the explosion woke him up. He straightened up in his seat on the bus as it pulled over in Stonewall.

Covering a yawn, he sat up and looked out the window. Watery autumn sunlight of mid-morning. A light rain was falling. People were walking down the sidewalk on errands.

Vince was within five miles of Mac Colls. He was looking forward to seeing Mac again…

He got up and made his way off the bus. There was a Walmart

on the edge of town. He would go there, buy some clean clothes, clean up in their bathroom, put the clothes on and get some breakfast at Pat's.

Then a long walk back to the cabin for the Desert Eagle. And the hike out to the Wolf Base.

Then…

He had to make a decision.

Should he try to take the place down now? Or should he try again to infiltrate—maybe just get Bobby out and run for it. Let Deirdre work with the FBI to take these bastards down. But that would come too late—wouldn't it?

Still unsure, Vince hurried down the street, wanting to change out of his cammies as quick as he could. He saw Sheriff Woodbridge drive by in his patrol car, staring at him. If Woodbridge chose to take a closer look, he might see the blood splashed on Vince's clothing. He'd got most of it rinsed off in the bus station bathroom, but there were some stubborn bloodstains a sharp-eyed observer could notice.

But the sheriff kept going and so did Vince.

Mid-afternoon now. The rain had ceased, the clouds rolled away, and mist rose, summoned by late-Autumn clouds. Wearing blue jeans, a long black and yellow plaid shirt, and a black vinyl jacket, all fresh from Walmart, Vince was trudging down the access road toward Wolf Base. He had the Desert Eagle under his new jacket and two pocketfuls of ammo. In his left hand was a Walmart bag stuffed with his dirty, blood-splashed paramilitary uniform.

He was operating under the assumption that Mac Colls, who seemed to hate him, had acted on his own. That Gustafson hadn't known that Colls planned to order Marco to take off. That Colls had taken a shot at him and had simply missed.

But he could be wrong. The General might have realized that Vince was not loyal to him and his cause. If that were the case, then Vince was walking into a wasp nest of enemies.

He had a strong feeling, however, that Gustafson wasn't in on the decision to leave him to the tender mercies of the local cops. Acting on that feeling was a gamble.

Vince also had a mounting sense that he was about to make a decision that would reshape his life.

Was he here for the right reasons? He did want to find Bobby Destry and set him free. But part of him wanted the fight. He knew that.

He had tried letting it all go—the warrior life, the soldier's life; the dependency on action and adrenaline to feel like life was worthwhile. Last year, he'd had a girlfriend for six months, up in Washington State.

Sandra June Tarkington. Till some drunk had tried to make a move on her in a bar. Vince told him to back off and the guy took a swing at Vince… who had broken the guy's wrist, and jaw, in under two seconds. He'd done it with such savagery it scared Sandra away.

She was never comfortable around him after that. She had muttered about soldiers with PTSD and then stopped taking his phone calls.

One way or another, if he kept walking down this road—literally and figuratively—he was going to find himself, in time, in violent confrontation with the Germanic Brethren. If he happened to kill one of them in a public place in self-defense, witnesses would probably clear him of wrongdoing. But it wasn't likely to play out that way. If he decided to go to war against them, he'd be breaking the law. He could become a wanted vigilante; an outsider, an outlaw in his own country.

Trouble was, he knew too much to back out now. *Firepower* was coming. He couldn't be sure Deirdre would be able to mobilize the FBI to stop it. There wasn't enough direct evidence. But Vince felt certain that innocent people would die if it weren't stopped. Maybe a lot of people.

That thought made up his mind for him.

Another quarter mile and Vince would come to the checkpoint. He could slip into the woods and go around it. But coming in that way they'd see him on one of their cameras, and some zealot might well take a shot at him. And he needed to look like he *belonged* here. That was the plan.

He kept striding on. Twenty minutes, and he rounded a curve to see the two guards and the gate blocking his way.

"Hello, Gunny," said Vince, strolling up to the checkpoint.

CHAPTER TEN

"You were issued a uniform," Gunny said, glaring at him with his one remaining eye.

"I have it here in the bag," Vince said. "There's blood on it. I should have gotten rid of it. But… I figured I might need it so Gustafson would have some kind of proof."

"Proof of what?" asked the other guard. It was the ex-con with tattoos up his neck, Dale French. Carrying an AR-15.

"That I carried out the mission. You two probably weren't briefed."

Gunny shook his head. "No, I wasn't. But you coming here like that—and on foot—no, you're not going through this gate without authorization from Mac."

Vince smiled grimly. "Mac? I could tell you a story about Mac Colls."

"What story's that?" French snorted.

Vince shook his head. "Not for your inky ears, kid."

"What'd you say to me, dude?" French said, starting to come around the gate.

Gunny reached out and grabbed French's arm, holding him back. "You try it, he'll wrap that rifle around your head."

Takes a professional to know one, Vince thought. Too bad he'd probably have to kill Gunny. The twisted old bastard.

Gunny was on his cell phone now. "Need you out here, Mac. Question about a man at the gate."

He broke the connection, and Vince put down the shopping bag.

"I should mention that I'm armed." He lifted his shirt to show the Desert Eagle.

French whistled. "That's a big damn pistol."

"Better leave that with me," Gunny said. "For now."

Vince thought about it. Then he nodded. "I guess it's protocol."

He tugged the big pistol out of his waistband and handed it across the gate to Gunny.

"Can I see it?" French said, putting his hand out.

"No," Gunny said, hefting the gun.

They waited, Vince with his arms crossed over his chest, whistling that old Jimi Hendrix song to himself.

A dark-green SUV came down the road from the base. Mac Colls was at the wheel. He pulled up just behind the checkpoint, got out, staring at Vince.

"You look surprised to see me, Sarge," Vince said mildly as Colls walked toward him, one hand on his holstered Glock.

Colls looked at the two guards. "You men leave us here—I need to talk to this man alone."

"My orders don't allow for that," Gunny said. "The General said—"

"This is coming from the General!" said Colls, drawing his pistol.

"You're lying, Mac," said Vince—and he vaulted over the gate, knocked Colls' gun hand aside, and hit him hard on the point of the chin with an uppercut.

Colls grunted and fell flat on his back, the gun still clutched in his hand. He was out cold.

"What the fuck!" French burst out.

As the two guards stared, still trying to wrap their heads around what had happened, Vince picked up Colls' gun, tossed it into the brush, and then lifted the unconscious man up. He slung Colls over his shoulder in a fireman's carry and toted him to the SUV.

"Gunny," French said, "we can't let him—I mean—"

"Stop right there, Bellator!" Gunny called.

"You two can shoot me down, but the General sent me on a mission and he's expecting me back, so you'd better think about explaining that to him," Vince said as he dumped Colls in the passenger seat of the SUV. He walked over to the open driver's side door and got in. The keys were in the ignition.

"Just wait here while I call it in!" Gunny shouted.

"I'll explain to the General in person!" Vince shouted, starting the car. He backed the SUV up, turning, swung around and floored it, roaring down the gravel road toward the base.

It took him about a minute to get there. The gates of the compound were open.

Vince pulled into the compound and up to the front door of the bunker complex. He turned off the engine and got out as a guard called to him from the fence.

"Hey—No one said you could—whoa there!"

Vince picked up the still slumbering Colls, carried him over his shoulder into the building, up the stairs—past Wynn Foster, who was gaping in amazement—and up to Gustafson's door. "General!" He called out. "It's Vincent Bellator! Little emergency here!"

Marco opened the door and Vince pushed past him, then

dumped the groaning Colls on the floor. He was beginning to wake up.

"Mac here had a mishap, sir," Vince said.

Gustafson, standing behind his desk, stared open-mouthed down at Colls. "What the devil is this?"

"It started with his taking a shot at me when I was coming back to exfil, and then taking off in the heli without me," Vince said. "Just now he tried to get me alone—and he had his gun in his hand. I left my gun and the bag with my uniform in it with Gunny Hansen."

"He hit me," Colls said, rubbing his jaw. He tried to sit up. "Sucker-punched me."

"If you let someone sucker-punch you, you don't know your job," Vince said.

Gustafson turned to Marco. "What's this about? I was told Bellator didn't come back from the mission!"

"Well—the sarge ordered me to take off," Marco said, wincing. "I *did* notice he took a shot at something through the door. But I didn't see who…"

"Stirner's men," Colls said, wobblingly sitting up. "Shot at them."

"There was no one left alive to follow me back," Vince said. "I killed them. Stirner too."

"We got word that Stirner and a group of men were killed," Gustafson said, sinking into his desk chair. "But… I don't know who to believe."

"I figured the Ragnarins killed Bellator and came after the helicopter," Marco said. "Because—why would the sarge shoot at Bellator?"

"Why indeed?" said Gustafson, looking at Colls.

"First he shot at me," Vince said, "and then he left me there and didn't pick up when I called from the burner. He figured it was his chance to get rid of me. Maybe he thinks I'm a rival. Maybe he's with the feds. I don't know why he did it, General. But I'm reporting in. Mission accomplished, sir."

"He's lying!" Colls snarled. He stood up, still unsteady.

"You hit him, Bellator, because—you said he pulled a gun on you? Where was this?"

"Out at the checkpoint. But I hit him because he deliberately took off with me right there in view—with no enemy around me. And he took a shot at me. I have a strong suspicion he wanted to get me away from Gunny and French and shoot me."

"Oh, bullshit, he was under arrest for coming in like that without reporting properly, without… without…"

Gustafson stared at Colls. "Mac—it seems to me the bullshit here is coming from you. You never said anything about having to shoot at anyone from that helicopter. You kept that from me. Well… it seems there's some enmity between you and Bellator here. Why is that?"

"I told you before, General—I don't trust him!" Mac snapped, jabbing a finger at Vince. "He hasn't been here long enough to be trusted!"

"The whole point of the mission," Vince said, "was for me to prove myself. Now I've done that. Half a dozen men are dead. I put my life and my freedom on the line for the Brethren!"

Gustafson nodded. "Seems that you did. And you succeeded in taking out Stirner. My judgment is this—Sergeant Colls here is on probation. He's been with me from the start and I'm not going to lose him now. He keeps out of your way, you keep out of his."

Vince nodded. It was as good as he could hope for. "Yes sir, that'll work for me—except there's one issue. He tried to kill me once already—maybe twice. He's got a gun. I don't have one. I have the right to bear arms, General. I want to carry my pistol. The one I left with Gunny Hansen."

"Who the hell does he think he is?" Colls asked in disbelief.

Gustafson took a deep breath. "Very well. I think you've earned it. And Mac's feelings aren't going to apply here. He seems to have deliberately compromised the end of the mission—"

"He's lying about that, sir!" Colls protested.

"Don't interrupt me! He gets his gun. Marco, you see to that."

"Yes sir."

"And Mac—leave my office! Go and get some ice for that swollen jaw. Decide if you need an X-Ray. Whatever you need to do. I'll talk to you later!"

"General—"

"You heard me, Sergeant!"

Colls growled, threw Vince a glance of burning hatred, and stalked out the door.

"Marco," said Gustafson, "go get that gun and bring it here. His uniform too. Inform Gunny of my decision. I want to talk to Bellator here alone."

"Yes sir."

Marco hurried out, closing the door behind him.

"Sit down, Vincent."

Vince sat across from the desk. He waited.

Gustafson gave him a slight smile. "Rather amusing, the way you carried Mac in here and tossed him on the floor like a sack of potatoes. But hereafter, treat him with respect. Despite everything. Maybe he'll learn to respect you in return."

Vince nodded gravely. Playing the part. "Yes sir."

"And remember—we have chain of command around here. We honor rank. He outranked you. From now on, you will honor rank if you intend to stay with us."

"Yes sir."

"We'll have to get you another uniform," Gustafson said. "I think we'll burn that one."

"Yes sir. There's blood on it."

Gustafson tented his fingers. "Vincent—the US military has made black and brown men a significant part of the armed forces. The Pentagon appoints black generals and it kowtows to the Jews. In fact—the Joint Chiefs are traitors to the white race. Which means they are traitors to the true America." He looked solemnly at Vince. "Do you agree?"

The irony of a highly treasonous man calling the military treasonous made Vince want to shake his head in amazement. But instead, he managed to reply with a reasonable facsimile of solemnity. "Yes sir. They are traitors."

"Good. I knew that was what was in your heart. The gods have told me so; the *Great God* has told me so!"

Vince didn't know how to reply to that. He just nodded in agreement.

Gustafson laced his fingers, leaned forward onto the desk and, almost whispering, he said, "I do things around here on a need-to-know basis, Vincent. You know the saying; three men can keep a secret if two of them are dead. We're not quite so rigid as that, but close. When Operation Firepower unfolds, there will be six separate groups of men responding from six regions of the country. None of them know their full role. Few of them know the full plan. In fact, most of these men know very little—only that it's a serious military action to be taken in D.C. They do know that they risk being killed or arrested. We've spent years getting men we could rely on, in those conditions. But they understand the need for secrecy. Hence, you'll understand, I cannot tell you everything." He took a deep breath and went on, "But I will tell you what *your* part in it is—at least, initially. On the day of the operation, your mission, Vincent, will be to go to a certain place, where the Joint Chiefs of Staff will be meeting with Defense Intelligence personnel. You will thereupon kill everyone in the room. You will assassinate the Joint Chiefs of Staff of the United States military…"

CHAPTER ELEVEN

"He wants you to do *what?*" Agent Deirdre Corlin had raised her voice a little, to go with her raised eyebrows.

Vince glanced nervously at the door of the library. No one seemed to be passing. He was back in Germanic Brethren uniform, but he felt he stuck out like a sore thumb after what had happened with Colls. "You heard right. The Joint Chiefs. I think he figures even if I failed, I'd create so much chaos at the Pentagon it'd be another one of the decoys he prizes. It'll draw more police and soldiers away from the real attack—and it'll make a 'Germanic Brethren' point of its own. I don't have a *when* or the target address. He's being cagey with that."

"I've got to report this as soon as I can…"

"You don't have to bring my name into it. Let's do that as little as possible. Just let 'em know it's planned."

She nodded. "It doesn't matter because we're not going to let *anyone* do it."

"I wonder how much he thinks he can really accomplish for his idiotic cause with all this," Vince murmured. "I mean, it's not as if—"

He broke off, hearing Wynn Foster and Shaun Adler talking in the hall outside the open door of the little library.

"I don't know when and I don't know where," Wynn was saying. "But we're doing it. And it's soon…"

They kept walking past the library. After he was sure they were gone, Vince whispered, "You find out anything?"

"I'm almost there. The guy you just heard saying he doesn't know? He knows. He's handling the dark web interface for the whole plan."

"You're using feminine wiles?"

"It's my way into his head," she said, sighing. "But he's not going to get lucky."

Vince smiled. Looking at this strong, admirable woman, crackling with intelligence and energy, he could almost daydream of getting lucky with her himself. But that daydream was something he didn't allow himself anymore.

Still—was there a sexual tension between him and Deirdre? He kind of thought there was.

"What's on your mind?" she asked suddenly.

"Me?" He was a little startled. "Nothing—I mean, everything. We need to know where and when and we need to know it soon, Deirdre. We need to be able to get into the emails, the directives, whatever's going out on the dark web."

She looked at him with her head cocked and her eyes narrowed, as if unsure of him. "I am still not committing to giving you what I find out. You're a loose cannon, Bellator."

"I delivered Stirner to your people. Even though someone should have wrung his neck."

"Do I want to know how you did it?"

"Probably not. Anyway, you're stuck with me. I'm here. I've still got to get Bobby out of that cell. And whatever they're planning—I'm not going to let it happen. Just tell me what you can. But I'll be more help if I know what's going on. All of it."

She shrugged. "I don't know. Maybe I should get permission. I'll be going out after mushrooms tomorrow. I'll make the call then."

"We've got some night training," Vince said. "I'd better get out there."

"Yeah, man, they're installing a minigun on that helicopter," Shaun Adler said as he and Vince moved into place in the woods. Each carrying an AR-15, they were trudging along in the trees around the range at the foot of the hill, both of them with night-seeing goggles on. The forest was an eerie shade of green and yellow through the night lenses. They could see the other men in their assigned approaches, coming from three directions to converge on the dozens of plywood outlines; silhouettes in the size and shape of men and women, set up in the center of the gun range area. They would converge their fire on the targets, and they were assigned to do it at shooting angles that weren't directly across from another shooter. That was the theory anyhow. Vince knew it could go badly wrong if someone screwed up.

The whole exercise gave Vince a sick feeling inside. Maybe this was just a rehearsal, but on a certain level, shit was getting real.

Because tonight they were practicing shooting into a crowd of people.

"What kind of minigun?" he asked. A "minigun" was not so mini. It was a very large and deadly serious machine gun. "NATO-style rotary miniguns?"

"Pretty much—an M134! I helped carry it up there—and the tools too. Marco's up there installing it with Gunny Hansen. Seems Gunny used them back in the Gulf War. They're having to cut into the deck and do some welding to retrofit that shit in there."

"That gun is old school. Vietnam era. Still some serious firepower to put on a civilian heli."

"Sure as hell is…"

The 7.62 x 51mm rotary machine gun was a kind of modern Gatling gun; its six barrels, driven by an electric motor, spun around and fired six-thousand rounds a minute. Devastating firepower…

A weapon like that in the hands of the Germanic Brethren, attached to a helicopter? The thought gave Vince a chill.

They reached their position marked with dayglow spray paint on a tree trunk and aimed their assault weapons. Vince waited for the signal.

A bullhorn voice called out, "Open fire!"

Fifteen men opened fire using three firing trajectories, their select-fire, auto-enabled AR-15s tearing into the wooden replicas. The night echoed with gunfire, an avalanche of racketing sound, muzzle flashes lit up yellow in the night-vision as the men fired and fired, .223 Remington rounds tearing the dummies to splinters…

These sons of bitches have to be stopped, Vince thought. Whatever it takes.

At lunch the next day, eating fried chicken and boiled vegetables, Vince glanced up to see Deirdre refilling his coffee cup. "Been to the library lately, Private Bellator?"

"No I have not. Any new books?"

"Yeah. You might want to pop in real quick after lunch. Something good came in."

She moved on and Shaun, sitting beside him, elbowed him and sniggered. "Dude you are so going to get some!"

"What, in the library?"

"That's just the start, man. She's so into you. 'Something good came in'. Yeah right!"

Vince shook his head. "We're just studying German together is all it is."

"That's how it starts, man."

"Listen to Mr. Experience here."

"Hey, you'd be surprised…"

"They get that minigun installed in the heli?"

Shaun nodded, ate a piece of pie, washed it down with some coffee, and said, "Yep. They worked most of the night and all this morning. All done. They got more ammunition than you can even imagine…"

Vince nodded. "Those things run through ammo quick. How they going to use it?"

"Do they tell me? It's need to know." He shrugged. "Seems like I don't need to know…"

But I do, Vince thought.

After he bussed his dishes he went to the library. Deirdre wasn't there. Edgy, thinking that undercover work wasn't his strength, Vince got out the Goethe, sat down, and pretended to study it.

Ten minutes passed, and Vince was startled when Gustafson came in, lips pursed, adjusting his glasses. "Ah—Vincent!" he said, crossing to the bookshelves. "Using your lunch hour well, I see."

"Still trying to get a handle on German. I took a little in school and it's starting to come back."

"*Klasse! Viel glück,* Vincent!"

"*Danke, mein herr.*"

Gustafson selected a thick book and bustled out with it.

Vincent realized his heart was pounding. He'd felt all day that something was in the air. Something dangerous was taking shape just out of his vantage point…

A few minutes later, Deirdre arrived, her cheeks red, her eyes glistening, and clearly in a hurry. She sat down across from him, on the edge of her seat. "I've got only half a minute," she murmured. "Listen—do you have a laptop?"

"Yes."

"I need something uploaded. I can't get away to do it. And I can't get at their systems here. Not anymore. I've been saving a pint of Jack and I got Wynn drunk last night. Got him to show off to me on the computer he uses to talk to the outlying Brethren. I sent him to bring me some water and he left the room, and I used a flash drive, copied a lot of email exchanges."

"He caught you?"

"Yeah. I'd just put the thing in my pocket and he saw what I had onscreen. He was pissed off I was 'snooping' and he won't let me in there again. Can't get in without a key."

"He suspect you?"

"I don't know. He was pretty woozy."

"They have their satellite internet but there's no regular wi-fi on the property here. I'd have to take the laptop into town to upload the stuff."

"Could you?"

"I could sneak out tonight, I guess."

She reached into a pocket, glanced at the door, then slipped him a flash drive and piece of paper. "Everything on it needs to go to that email."

He nodded, pocketing the slip of paper and flash drive. "See what I can do."

"I guess—what's to stop you from looking at what's on there. But I didn't give you permission. Right?"

"Right."

Deirdre nodded, got up, and then surprised him by reaching out and putting her hand on his. "Be really careful. I mean—*very*."

"Count on it."

She got up and left without another word. Vince sat there, leafing through the Goethe, thinking that he really wanted to look at what was on that flash drive. But it was too dangerous to do it here on base…

He'd do it tonight, when he slipped away to town. If they realized he was AWOL and called him out for it later, he'd say he went off to see a girl, or get a drink, or both.

But he still had that nagging hunch…

Something was smoldering—and about to burst into flame.

Mac Colls was walking down the hall with Marco Ambra. "You better get geared up for training, Corporal," Colls said.

"I'm on my way to the locker, Sarge."

That's when Vincent Bellator stepped out of the library up ahead. Bellator ignored them and walked off toward the lockers. Colls glared knives into Bellator's back but kept quiet. The

General insisted he was keeping Bellator in the dark about most of Firepower. Still—Colls felt like the guy was hiding something. And he'd sucker-punched Colls; humiliated him in front of the General. Bellator had to go down. But Colls would need some kind of proof against him…

Colls and Ambra passed the open library door—and they both glanced in, seeing Deirdre Corlin just getting up from a reading table.

"Ha!" murmured Ambra.

"'Ha' *what*, Corporal?" Colls asked as they walked by.

"I saw those two meet in there another time—I figure Bellator's making his move on her. Maybe they got a—what d'you call it—a tryst planned. You know? I don't blame him."

"So they've been meeting in there?"

"Seemed like to me."

They reached the stairs and Colls said, "Corporal—I've forgotten something in my office. I'll see you out there."

"See you there, Sarge."

Colls turned back and strode quickly to the library—where he met Deirdre leaving. "Hey—Shield Maiden Corlin. You having meetings with Bellator? Right now we've got a ban on our people getting frisky with each other."

Her face went blank—a little too blank. "Not sure what you mean, Sergeant."

"I hear you and he are hanging out in there together. We don't use the library for socializing."

She shook her head. "He's come in, once or twice, while I was studying."

"Yeah? Studying what?"

"German. You'll have to excuse me—I need to get a grounds permission from the General."

"What for?"

"Mushrooms, herbs—his cook needs them."

"So—out in the woods?"

"They don't grow on the carpet, Sergeant."

"Don't get smartassed with me, woman."

She shrugged. "Sorry. Just—like to keep a sense of humor. Okay if I go see the General now?"

"When's your big mushroom expedition?"

"Maybe this afternoon if I have time."

"Just see you get it done and get back into the building, with all dispatch."

She nodded and gave him a salute and a polite smile and walked toward the General's offices.

Colls stared after her. *She meets with Bellator. Tomorrow she's going out to the woods. Romantic assignation, mushroom hunting—or something else?* She'd kept her cool, but Colls felt he'd seen a caught look in her eye when he stopped her outside the library.

If Bellator was a quisling, and he was meeting with her, maybe she was a traitor too...

Halfway through the afternoon, Vince was out on the range with Shaun, watching the young man shoot. A motion from the west caught Vince's attention and he turned to see a team of Germanic Brethren escorting Agent Deirdre Corlin from the woods.

It was Mac Colls, Dale French, Gunny Hansen, and Marco Ambra, herding her along. They were about a hundred yards away, striding through a field of ferns. Her hands were behind her, probably cuffed. She stared fixedly ahead, affecting a look of puzzlement.

Vince guessed someone had followed her out to the satphone. French and Marco were carrying the aluminum box, between them, that she'd stashed in the woods. Meaning they'd found her satellite phone, her gun, and whatever else was in that box. Maybe more Jack Daniels for "trading with the natives".

Pistol in hand pointed at Deirdre's back, Colls had a look of surly triumph on his face.

Suddenly tautly aware of the gunshots cracking at the range, of eight men firing at the targets against the hill, Vince asked himself what the hell he was going to do now.

Must be someone—Colls, judging by his smug expression—had heard Deirdre talking in the library. They'd thought themselves talking in voices too low to be heard. But from bad timing, or a trick of acoustics they hadn't counted on, they'd been overheard.

This is my fault, Vince told himself bitterly. I should never have suggested we meet anywhere in the building. But both of them getting away to the woods to meet had seemed problematic.

Excuses.

If they'd heard her talking in the library, they heard who she was talking to, Vince realized.

He moved off to Shaun's left so that the bole of a big fir tree blocked him from Colls' view. Soon enough, Colls would be coming after Vincent Bellator with every resource at his disposal. Gustafson would give him permission once he heard the revelation about Deirdre. *"Deirdre Johansen' is not Deirdre Johansen... She's a federal agent."*

Would they cancel Operation Firepower because there was a federal agent amongst them?

Doubtful. From the hints Gustafson had dropped, they would simply give the signal and send all the Brethren cells in to attack D.C. While Gustafson, likely, split for cover somewhere.

She'd stall them with some kind of story. But Vince very much doubted it would work. And they would come for him next.

The question was, what was he going to do about it?

He glanced at the men on the firing range. Rocky Chesterton was there, teaching the other men. Shaun was popping away with a carbine. Vince had his Desert Eagle with him, had the jump on them, and he might be able to kill most of them, but there were a lot of men there with automatic and semi-auto weapons and it was broad daylight.

He could slip away—but if he did, he'd leave Deirdre at their mercy. He suspected they wouldn't kill her right away. Gustafson would want time to think it through, possibly keep her as a hostage.

At some point, they would kill her. They'd probably make it look like an accident somewhere away from the base.

Don't delay, he told himself. Within an hour, Mac will be out here with his men looking for you. This wasn't the time for a firefight. Have to get that message to the feds.

But there was no way he was simply leaving Deirdre Corlin and Bobby Destry here. Not for long.

He could get to town and call the FBI, tell them what had happened.

And how long would it take the feds to decide he was telling the truth? How long to get a raid organized? What would happen to Deirdre and Bobby in the meanwhile?

He couldn't wait for the feds. But neither could he make his move right this second.

Vince leaned over, looked around the big tree. He could see Colls and the others in the distance, their backs to him, still marching Deirdre toward the base.

He could go after Deirdre's escort and kill them all. But that'd bring hell down on him and Deirdre from everyone else on the base. They'd be out in the open.

He shook his head. First things first. Get off the base.

"Hey Shaun," he said.

Shaun got up and turned to him. "How'm I doing, Vince?"

"Great. I'd hate to be on the wrong end of that gun. Listen." He took a deep breath, then put a hand on Shaun's shoulder, leaned near the young man and spoke right in his ear. "You need to think about leaving here. If there's any shooting, anything going down… *Get out*. Head through the woods for town."

Shaun stepped back and gaped at him. "What!"

"Stay chill, Shaun. Just think about what I said. I'm not fucking with you. You want to help Bobby, right?"

"Yeah, but…"

"Then stay alive and out of jail. That means leaving here first chance you get. Even before any trouble, if you're smart. I'm going to get Bobby out of here. But I won't be able to watch your back."

"Oh Jesus. Does this mean what I think it means?"

"Don't ask. Just promise me you won't say anything to anyone. For Bobby's sake. At least for today." He extended his hand to Shaun. "Is it a deal?"

Shaun hesitated. Guns cracked and rattled nearby.

Then Shaun took his hand. "I guess so. For Bobby. But what are you going to do?"

Vince smiled and said, "I'm going to take a piss."

"You're going to…?"

"Yeah. I'm going off in the brush to take a piss. We all do it sometimes, out here. I'm going to do that right now, Shaun. And you're going to finish your clip out on that target and think about what I told you—about what to do when things get ugly out here."

Vince winked at him and turned away, strode into the brush. He headed off to the northwest, looking for the blaze he'd made on a scrub oak.

There it was. He ran to it, dug the pack from under the dry leaves. It had his laptop and the flash drive in it. He slung it over his shoulder, then strode toward the Brethren compound.

He'd made up his mind he'd need the Harley. Time was a serious consideration.

By the time he got to the compound, Mac and the others escorting Deirdre had gone into the building. The guards on the walls paid no attention to him as he strode up, pack over one shoulder; thus far, no alert had gone out about Vincent Bellator. But he knew it was coming.

Vince walked confidently up to his motorcycle, took the keys from the bag, put the little pack in the bike's saddlebags, climbed onto the bike, started the engine, and rode out from through the gates.

He thought he heard someone call after him but he ignored them.

Vince rode flat-out down the road, then slowed, turning off before coming in sight of the checkpoint. He rode down a game trail, weaving his way between trees, having to go fairly slowly to get around obstacles. Once he had to lift the bike over a fallen log.

He found a dry wash heading west and rode down that past the two gates, then worked his way back up to the access road. Soon he was on the highway, riding for Stonewall. He headed there with all the speed he could manage while still making the curves.

He was wondering if he'd made a mistake telling Shaun to get out; basically letting him know that Vince Bellator was no Germanic Brethren. Maybe Shaun would decide to be a stand-up, true-blue domestic terrorist and run to Gustafson with the information.

But—he had saved Shaun's hide in Tina's. He'd seemed willing to trust Vince ever since.

Vince turned off just before town and rode out to the cabin. He parked the bike outside and looked the place over. It didn't seem to have been disturbed.

He changed his clothes there, getting rid of the hated paramilitary uniform, got back on the Harley and rode to Pat's, where he knew there was wi-wi.

Sitting in a corner booth, with coffee and pie, he immediately accessed the flash drive. He glanced through it, confirmed she had found what she'd been looking for, and uploaded it to the email Deirdre had given him, along with an advisory about what had happened to Agent Deirdre Corlin.

Then he read his own copy of the documents…

And the pieces began to come together.

CHAPTER TWELVE

"You can start by telling us what your real name is," said Mac Colls.

"It's Deirdre Cynthia Johansen," she said, in a fair imitation of exasperation. "This is stupid... You know me... I've been with the Brethren for more than a year!"

She was standing in front of Gustafson's desk, her hands bound behind her with plastic police ties. Mac was standing to one side, Marco on the other. It was two hours after the federal agent had been captured, and Mac was frustrated that no movement had been made on Vincent Bellator and that, after cooling her heels a while in one of the basement cells, "Deirdre Johansen" was just now being interrogated by General Gustafson.

Gustafson was scowling, chewing up a Tums for an acid stomach as he looked at a printout in front of him. "Answer Mac's question," the General said. "What's your real name?"

She shook her head sadly. "General—you don't understand. I was bothered by not being able to stay in touch with my family, out here. My mother is sick, my brother was having problems, I have a fiancé—I needed to stay in touch with people. A forty-day stretch here without a phone was just not doable. So I got the satphone. And the gun—I'm just careful, that's all. You don't usually let Shield Maidens carry a gun."

"We called the recent numbers used on that phone," Gustafson said. "The numbers didn't connect all the way—they required a code input to go through. A code we don't have. What family does that?"

"Mine does, sir! We have trouble with harassment because of our views. You should understand that."

Gustafson shrugged. "I just thought I'd see what story you'd tell us. You see, you have a serial number on that gun. We called in a favor… and traced it. It's an FBI issue gun. And the satellite phone you use is standard for agents in the field in remote places. It's the exact model used by the FBI."

Mac put in, "And she was meeting with Bellator in the library, sir. More than once, the way I've heard it He's with her on this, General!"

Gustafson frowned at him, looked like he was about to demur—then he winced. "Yes. It's quite possible." The General looked the FBI agent in the eyes and she looked back at him with bland defiance. "You won't tell us your name?"

"I don't know what you're talking about."

Gustafson turned the printout on his desk to face her. She saw her own face looking back at her from the file print. "The gun is registered to Deirdre Corlin, FBI. I could have led with that but—I just wanted to know if you were going to tell us without coercion. A little preview of what is to come. It appears coercion will be necessary. How about this question—is Vincent Bellator a federal agent?"

"No," she said. "He's what he seems to be. A professional soldier."

"And what have you learned about us and who precisely did you tell it to?"

She hesitated, looked at the picture on the printout again, then said, "I am Deirdre Elizabeth Corlin, a federal officer of the Justice Department, FBI badge number eight-two-seven-seven-one. I can now apprise you that you are under arrest for sedition and for the abduction and restraint of a federal officer. Your best bet is to release me and come with me to town, where I can arrange for you to call your lawyer. You can then turn yourself in at—"

She was interrupted by laughter—Mac Colls and Marco were both laughing, now. Gustafson was smiling crookedly. "Quite a performance, Miss Corlin. Men, take her to the available cell, and lock her up. We'll give her some time to think things over. Then we'll begin the interrogation. As to what we'll do with her after that—it really depends on her."

"What about Bellator, sir?" Mac asked.

"Once you have this woman in the cell, tell Gunny to have Bellator brought in and taken into custody. Gunny had better get a lot of help to do that. You go with him. Only shoot Bellator if necessary."

"Suppose Bellator left the base?"

"Then take some men, find him, and kill him—as discreetly as possible. We can take no chances…"

It was all there, in a set of emails to six correspondents. The dark web isn't always so dark.

The plans for the attack, discussed with the handful of men allowed to know.

There was more—Gustafson had sent an email to a source

in Russia, advising him that he may need exfiltration. Professor Gustafson assured the source that the SVR would not have to support him once he was in Russia. He had most of his money in a Swiss bank account.

Did that mean Gustafson was a Russian agent?

But as he read on, it sounded as if the Russians were more like Gustafson's allies. There were strong white nationalist undercurrents in Russia, all tangled with a hyper-right-wing version of Russian Orthodox Christianity. Still, Russian intelligence services were always delighted at any domestic terrorism chaos in the USA. They were happy to help…

The attack was laid out in one email with "FOR YOUR EYES ONLY" in the subject line. It was to take place in less than twenty-four hours.

Nine-thirty tomorrow morning.

Six cadres of Germanic Brethren from around the country were already in the D.C. area. There were twenty men in each cadre, a hundred twenty total. They would come in six trucks—trucks rebuilt from junkyard vehicles, with false license plates—and converge on the senatorial event at the Lincoln Memorial.

Three other attacks, with individual operatives, were to take place shortly before the big one—an attack on the Joint Chiefs, a suicide bomber attack at a central police station, and an attack on a site to be decided at the last moment. All three men to draw police presence away from the main attack.

Vince pored over the emails again and again and found no clues to the third decoy attack.

He looked to see if he'd gotten a reply from the email he'd sent to the FBI agent.

Nope.

He remembered Gustafson's references to having someone inside the system. What if—

"Would you like another beer?" came a chirpy voice at his elbow.

Startled, he looked up to see the pretty black-haired waitress smiling at him. He thought he saw an invitation in her eyes for something more than beer.

Vince wished he could put it all aside and say yes to that question in her eyes. Just get lost in her arms and forget who he was and what he had to do.

But he said, "I'll have a cup of coffee and a cheeseburger with everything you can possibly put on it." He smiled at her. "Got work to do—and I won't have time for dinner…"

"Your simple mistake, right now, Agent Corlin, is that you think someone's going to get you out of this," Gustafson said.

He was standing near the door of the cell, looking frankly, even pityingly, at her. Mac Colls was leaning against the wall, arms crossed, watching Corlin. She was sitting on her bunk, in a corner, her drawn-up knees clasped by her arms. She had a brave face but her body language said she was scared.

Mac wondered when they'd start actual physical pressure in the interrogation process. To him it seemed obvious that all this talk wasn't going to work. The water treatment was a better move. Or just beat the crap out of her for an hour or so. She was a traitor to her race—she deserved it.

"But you see, Agent Corlin," said Gustafson, "we've got friends in the Justice Department. They're more than friends. We also have them in Defense. The Brethren are more highly placed than you

144

realize. At this point, several persons whom you were in contact with have been detained. Any calls about attacks on Washington in the next twenty-four hours will be blocked from going up the chain of command. It's all been arranged. It doesn't matter what Bellator tells people—he does not appear to be a federal agent. He has no standing. False warnings about attacks happen every day, you know. Anything he says will be dismissed."

"And we'll have him dead and in the ground in an hour or two," Mac said.

Gustafson raised his hand for quiet. "Miss Corlin—it's time for you to answer our questions. How much did you find out about our plans?"

"I tried very hard—and found out very little," she said, shrugging. "I heard the term Operation Firepower—but no sense of where and when and what it is exactly."

Gustafson snorted. "I think you're lying. We're going to have to get rough with you fairly soon. I have matters to arrange, but I shall be back and I *will* have my questions answered."

"You think you're not going to be in jail after all this?" she asked. "Really? Are you megalomaniacal enough to be that much in denial?"

"Do not mistake a deep-seated sense of duty to my own people for megalomania. As for denial—I know the risks. I have my own… preparations." He gave her a wry smile. "No need to be concerned for my sake."

"These people in government who are supposedly protecting you—they must be low level."

He shook his head. "You're not going to draw me out that way."

She shrugged. "What can they hope to gain, I wonder? An

attack will just make the nation more fully prepared to take your kind down."

"This attack will be a signal for true patriots to arise from many places. Including the United States military… and the nation's police departments."

"I doubt it. The 'Big Boogaloo' won't happen. You're deluded, Gustafson—and you'll be taking people like poor Mac Colls here down with you."

"Let me deal with her," Mac said, seething at her condescension toward him.

"Oh, you'll have your chance if she doesn't cooperate," Gustafson said. "We'll start with a form of torture you can *survive*—and move on from there. It's a shame—she could be exchanged for one of our people, perhaps, at some later date, were she to cooperate. But with this kind of resistance—I doubt she'll survive the interrogation."

He turned and went through the door. Mac threw a final contemptuous glance at Corlin, then followed Gustafson. He turned the key in the lock and glanced through the small barred window in the door. She waved at him cheerfully, then lay back on the cot, hands behind her head, smiling.

It's all an act, he told himself, turning angrily away. I'll remember that sneering smile—when she's screaming.

Vince rode up to the base of the rock formation, south of the Wolf Base. He switched off the bike and pushed it to a sheltered place between two boulders.

Then he went to stand on the edge of the cliff at the foot of the formation. He was wearing jeans, his own Rangers boots, a t-shirt, and his brown leather jacket. Around his hips was the army-surplus belt he'd taken from the Brethren, which held the holsters for his knife and pistol. On his back was the small pack, containing a flashlight, two bottles of water and an energy bar bought at a gas station, and sixty rounds of .50 Action Express ammunition.

He was looking north, at the ridge, the escarpment containing the Brethren's bunker complex.

He'd spent two hours poring over maps and Google satellite images of the region around Stonewall and the Wolf Base, and it was dusk when he rode up to Sullivan Rock. The rock formation, part of the National Forest, reminded some people of a soldier facing the world from a high ridge. Carved by nature in sandstone, it reared gray-red over a shallow valley, across from the ridge containing the underground bunker complex. Wolf Base was almost two miles off, blurred by autumn mist and the smoke drifting in from fireplace chimneys around Stonewall.

Optimum tactics required Vince to make his approach from above the base. There were no clear-cut overland approaches he could take to the ridgetop on a motorcycle. The creviced northern end of the ridge was open ground, with no cover, and there were security cameras watching it. Assuming the sheer cliff would prevent intruders from the east, Gustafson had set up no security cams looking toward the back of the base.

Vince had hoped to hear police sirens by now. He'd left messages with a tip line at the FBI—he'd been unable to get through to an agent—and he'd sent a number of emails. He'd even filled out tip forms online. He had thought about calling the Sheriff—but Shaun had said Woodbridge was friendly with Gustafson and he'd been seen at Wolf Base more than once. He couldn't be trusted.

Vince had thought about the State Police, too—but they'd just send a patrol car who'd ask around at the base if there was an Agent Corlin there. They would get a puzzled "no". And they wouldn't obtain a search warrant on his say-so. Not today.

Until the FBI got off the dime, he was going to have to handle this himself.

And he was going to have to walk there to do it…

He looked at the sky. There was a thin cloud cover; a nearly full moon was rising at the horizon.

Armed with the Desert Eagle and a knife, Vince started down the hillside, following a path that looked like it had been made by a mountain goat—it probably had. He was soon skidding down between stunted trees, catching hold of a branch now and then to keep from plunging headlong down the steep slope.

A few minutes later he came to an outcropping of granite, climbed down it, then descended along a zig-zag trail to the valley floor.

Vince started across, heading for the eastern side of the ridge. This was going to take a while… and the shadows were growing long.

Passing through several meadows of ferns ringed by pines, he came to a stream that ran south behind the Wolf Base ridge. A thin, intermittent hunter's trail ran alongside the stream. He followed the spotty trail alongside the gurgling stream. When the trail vanished into thick underbrush, he found a way around atop the boulders edging the creek. Mosquitoes were out in clouds, here, swarming in the twilight. He climbed down to a muddy bank of the stream and smeared mud on his face, neck and hands. It would be a help blending into the night and it'd keep the mosquitoes to a minimum.

He trudged on, as the darkness thickened around him. In the thin moonlight he could see silhouettes of branches in his way and the lineaments of the rocky, irregular trail.

He wasn't sure how much time passed as he traipsed north, but it felt like two hours when the tree cover broke up, opened by an ancient fall of rocks now half imbedded in the earth. The back of the rocky escarpment rose before him, twice as high as the highest tree in the woods.

He had done a lot of rock climbing and cliff scaling with the Rangers, and Vince thought he could probably find a way up the escarpment. But it occurred to him, looking up, that he might have been overconfident. A lot of this looked sheer. And it was damp out. The rocks could be slippery. It was getting dark and he had no climbing gear. He was going to have to free-climb.

Vince didn't like the odds. But he was committed now.

He took off his backpack, methodically ate the energy bar, and drank half a bottle of water, all the while looking at the cliffside for the best climbing route. He got his small flashlight from the pack, put the pack back on, and used the flashlight to work his way across the craggy fallen boulders toward the foot of the cliff.

A bat fluttered overhead, and crickets sawed at the air with their calls. Still no sirens.

Jumping from rock to rock, Vince reached the debris of stone and desiccated wood at the base of the cliff. He climbed the pile of debris to the cliff face and found the long vertical crack he'd spotted at the corner of the escarpment. He looked it over for a few seconds, using the flashlight where it was hard to make out. Then he put the flashlight in a coat pocket and started to climb…

CHAPTER THIRTEEN

Agent Deirdre Corlin raised her dripping head from the aluminum washtub. She managed to keep that annoying, flinty expression on her face, Mac noticed.

French still had his hand on the back of her neck. Her hands were plastic-cuffed behind her.

"Well, agent?" said Mac. "You want to go through that until you croak, or do you want to tell us?"

"I did tell you," Agent Corlin said, coughing. "I only found out the name. I tried to get people to talk about it but the General was too careful about need-to-know. And locking doors."

"You were going to report something—I heard you say so. What was it?"

"Just that there were some night drills." She coughed again. "Which suggested it might happen at night."

"That wasn't what you were talking about in the library. I heard you! It was something urgent!"

"I was thinking of asking to transfer out of the mission. That was urgent for me. I was fed up feeding and caring for ignorant, brainwashed scumbags."

French snarled at that. Not waiting for Mac's order, he shoved her head back under the water. She squirmed and fought, trying to straighten up.

"Let her up," he said.

"She's a—"

"Let her up!"

"Well, shit, Mac." French let her straighten up. She gasped and coughed as he went on. "We're not going to get anywhere that way. You got to take her right to the edge. It's panic that does it. I saw it on a Tv show."

"You're wasting your energy," she sputtered. She coughed up water and said, hoarsely, "Should be deciding how to turn yourself in. Get the best deal."

"Oh the hell with this…" French muttered. He stood up and unbuckled his pants. "I'm gonna take some of the high and mighty out of her." He unzipped his pants—

And she twisted herself to the right and kicked back at him, driving the heel of her right foot up into French's crotch, straight into his balls.

French squealed with pain—a funny sound to come out of so big a man—and Mac had to smile. "She did you a good—"

Mac didn't get the rest out because she kicked him in the solar plexus. He gasped and stepped quickly back, wheezing.

"Bitch, I'm gonna kick her ass for this," French said, his voice still high.

Then came the sound of a key turning in the lock. The door opened and Gustafson came in, carrying a short coil of rope. "What the devil are you doing with your pants open like that, French?" he demanded.

"Sir," French said. "She was being so uppity—she kicked me in the nuts—"

"Then I won't have to! Zip up your pants and get out of the way. Sergeant, take this." Gustafson tossed Colls the rope. "Tie that to her wrists and run the other end through the bars in the door."

Still getting his breath, Mac did as he was ordered—French had to hold the squirming agent down so he could tie the rope on.

Gustafson nodded. "Fine. Now hoist her up."

French pulled the rope hand-over-hand so that she was lifted to her tiptoes by the knot around her wrists, pulling her arms into a brutally unnatural position. She groaned, and clenched her eyes shut.

"French, tie the other end to the cot." The metal legs of the cots were bolted to the floor. French tied the rope to a steel leg, making sure the rope was taut.

"Okay, we leave her there for a while," said Gustafson. "Unless you have some fresh information for us, Miss Corlin?"

"Fuck you, assholes!" grated Agent Corlin.

"I see. Come on, men. We'll lock the door and leave her dangling from it. We have a planning session to go to in the conference room… Back in an hour, perhaps, Miss Corlin."

"Don't bother!" she shouted hoarsely.

She moaned in pain when they swung the door closed.

The wind rose, trying to push Vince off the escarpment. It soughed off the stone and spattered him with intermittent rain.

And he was stuck.

Vince had gotten himself boxed into a corner, hundreds of feet over the foot of the cliff. The darkness had fooled him. When he got to the lip of the cliff, at the top of the crack he'd been using for footholds, he found a boulder beetled over him, right in his way. It was jutting out too far for him to reach over. If he tried, he'd fall.

Now what?

He held on with his left hand and his feet and reached into his coat with his right hand, tugging out the flashlight. He switched on the light and shone it at the rockfaces to the left and right of him. To the left it was sheer. Not a handhold in sight. To the right—the same.

But when he tried again over to the right, moving the light more slowly, the oblong glow of the light played over a recess in the rock, *almost* within reach. If he could grab it with his right hand, maybe it'd hold him long enough so that he could grab the upper edge of the cliff with his left, where the cliff's lip was flatter. But that would require lunging for that recess. There was a very good chance he wouldn't be able to hold on even if he caught it.

He could climb back down and try to find another route. But what was happening to Deirdre Corlin, meanwhile?

You're a Ranger, he told himself. Focus, and bring all of your attention to this, and you can do it.

Vince took a deep breath, leaned in as close to the rock wall as he could, memorizing the exact position of that recess. He flicked the flashlight off, slipped it in his pocket, stretched out his right arm—and lunged at the handhold.

He slapped his right hand down into it—and felt the water coating it, his fingers slipping…

He clapped his left hand down on the upper lip of the cliff… and it caught a rocky knob. His right slipped from the recess and he fell with a jerk to the end of his left arm…

He ground his teeth with pain and thrashed with his right hand at the recess. He felt for a foothold and the toe of his right boot caught a tiny ledge. It held his weight and he was able to lift up half an inch and slap his right hand into the recess. He did a crooked pull-up, feeling close to tearing a muscle. There was a roaring in his ears. The wind tugged at him—then he slapped at the lip of the cliff with his right hand, and caught hold. Now he could do a regulation pull-up. He grunted, feeling the gravitational pull of the world dragging at him like a living thing as he pulled himself up to the edge.

An agonizing three seconds—until his chin was level with the top. He lashed his right hand out, found a crack in the stone, gripped, and pulled, clambering with his feet…

And then he was crawling over the edge, onto the top of the cliff.

Vince lay there panting for ten long seconds.

You're a damned fool, Bellator, he told himself. But so far, still alive.

He got to his knees and glanced around. The top of the ridge in this area was ruggedly flat, like a modest plateau. No one was in sight. But he could see the hulking shape of the camouflaged helicopter about fifty yards away.

Vince got up, wiped sweat from his forehead, unsheathed his knife, and started for the heli, thinking he could use it as cover to get nearer the emplacements.

Then he stopped. It occurred to him that they might have surveillance cameras around the chopper.

He changed direction, heading south on the uneven stone of the escarpment's top, trying to move as quietly as he could.

Much of it was cracked, pebbly granite, broken up by red-barked shrubs and witch hazel. As he moved to the west, he spotted the hump-shapes of the concrete and steel emplacements up ahead, still some distance off.

The witch hazel—shrubby trees—grew thickly closer to the emplacements. He moved in a crouch, using clumps of the small trees as cover, picking his steps as carefully as he could in the frail light.

He stopped from time to time, listening and looking. He heard men's voices, the words unintelligible, but the timbre hinting of casual conversation. He saw no cameras pointed his way.

Vince eased forward, seeing a pool of light from the back of the emplacement. The gun battery was a low, semi cupola of reinforced concrete, with gun slits in the western side for light machine guns and sniper rifles. The interior was recessed into the top of the ridge, bunker-style; the back was open, with green tarps that could be hooked to the back of the opening in case of heavy rain. He was glad the rain had stopped. If the tarp had covered the back entrance to the emplacement it would have complicated matters.

As he got closer—fifty feet away—he could see two men in paramilitary uniforms sitting on benches to either side of the guns. One short, one taller, both crewcut white guys. They had a shelf of equipment handy. Vince couldn't see it clearly, but he figured the gear was binoculars and night-seeing goggles. The militiamen were sitting facing one another, eating sandwiches and talking.

Vince planned to kill them silently if he could. Unnecessary gunfire would alert the other emplacement, maybe the whole compound.

Knife in hand, he stole yet closer, keeping to the south so that the man on the left would be unable to see him approach. At twenty feet off, he could hear what they were saying. "So Herb says, 'There's two uses for liberals, and one of them is sucking dick.'"

This was apparently a punchline, as both men burst into raucous laughter. Vince used the noise to creep up even closer. He switched his knife to his left hand, holding it by the blade, then took the Desert Eagle in his right, holding it by the barrel.

"One time I was in this bar in Vancouver, Washington, place called the Ice House, and we—"

The man broke off, staring, as Vince jumped down into the cupola and threw the knife with his left hand at the man across from him. It sped true, and bisected the militiaman's throat, right through the voice box—something Vince only saw peripherally as he spun to his left and brought down the pistol's butt hard on the other man's forehead. Hard enough to smash it in so that blood and brains spurted and the man crumpled, dead in under a second.

Vince stepped back to avoid the blood, frowning to find some of it had gotten on the bottom of the seven-round clip in the Desert Eagle.

He knelt by the dead man's legs and used the corpse's trouser cuffs to carefully wipe the blood off the clip of the big pistol. Blood drained from the bodies and down the flood drain in the concrete floor of the emplacement.

Retrieving his knife, he wiped it off and took one of the night-seeing SWIR devices from the shelf. He hung them from his belt, then began moving across the terrain toward the other emplacement, staying west enough that they wouldn't likely spot him.

Vince was aware on some level that he'd shifted into a certain highly specialized state of mind. It was a state of heightened acuity; of taut reflexes and crystalline objectivity. His pulse was up and he tasted metal in his mouth. But it wasn't from fear. It was the watchful intensity of a professional warrior. It was the mental and physical state of a specialist.

He started moving faster, almost running, not wanting to be caught in the open if one of them spotted him. In a minute he'd reached the igloo-like curve of the second emplacement's semi-dome—and then one of the men chose that moment to step up onto the ridge for a cigarette.

The unlit cigarette dangling from his lips, the gangly militiaman stared in shock, seeing Vince. He opened his mouth to shout and only got a gurgle out as Vince's spinning knife buried itself in his throat.

But a second man, powerfully muscled and thick-necked, blurted, "Son of a *bitch!*" and pulled his pistol as Vince turned to him. Vince had been planning to use the Desert Eagle as a hammer again; now he had to reverse the gun in his hand, which took half a second, and the man had time to get off a shot. The bullet cracked by Vince's head, and he fired back—the big Desert Eagle .50 round slamming into the militiaman's breast bone. The man went staggering back, his face contorted by pain and fear. He fell onto his back, over the steel trapdoor that led to the lower levels.

The bullet had passed through the body-builder and into the concrete wall, punching deeply between the gun slits. The .50 was a powerful load in a powerful handgun.

Wondering if anyone had heard the shot down below, Vince holstered his gun, retrieved his knife, cleaned and sheathed it.

He noticed a select-fire extended clip AR-15 leaning against the wall. Why not?

He dragged the muscle-builder off the trap door —the big guy's dead weight took some real effort to move. He found the trap door locked.

Vince dug in the pockets of the dead man, came up with a small ring of keys. He unlocked the trap door, lifted it up a few inches and peered through. He could see the empty top-flight of the stairs, lit by a dull-yellow overhead light. He listened and heard nothing from below. He opened the trap door the rest of the way, pocketed the keys, took the AR-15, slinging its rifle strap over one shoulder, and climbed down the ladder.

He took the assault rifle into his hands, checked the clip—it was fully loaded—and set the fire to semi-auto. Then he started down the stairs, reviewing the top floor in his mind. There was the upstairs barracks to the south, but there would likely be no one in it. Everyone bunked in the first-floor barracks. At this hour there might still be Brethren lingering in the cafeteria and kitchen, also on the top floor. Most of the base's troops would be done with dinner and probably in the downstairs barracks, prepping for training.

Vince hoped he didn't have to kill the two Brethren-loyal Shield Maidens. Or Shaun Adler.

The alert would have gone out on him. He'd probably have to kill anyone he encountered. If Deirdre were still alive she'd probably be down in a basement cell or in Gustafson's office. And that office would be Vince's first stop.

Vince reached the third floor, stepped through the door from the stairway—and immediately saw Rocky Chesterton, coming down the corridor from his right.

Rocky was a craggy-faced man, tall and wide-shouldered and deft in his movements. And he was raising his Glock—but as he was doing that, Vince was aiming.

Vince squeezed off an AR-15 round and it caught Rocky in the forehead. The man's head jerked back and he convulsively squeezed the Glock's trigger. The bullet spanged off a metal brace in the wall and cut through a corner of Vince's leather jacket, just missing his waist.

Three shots, one ricochet. So much for stealth, Vince thought.

Rocky fell, and gun smoke swirled in the corridor. Behind Vince was the empty barracks; ahead was the cafeteria and kitchen. Past that, the administration offices and comm center.

He got ten steps down the corridor and saw a man's head sticking out of a doorway; one of the Brethren looking nervously around. Vince had heard the red-haired guy called Smitty.

Vince fired from the hip, missing, and Smitty ducked back in the cafeteria. He slammed the door shut. Vince heard the door locking.

Vince started jogging now, passing the cafeteria door, hearing shouting from inside. He reached the L-turn in the corridor that would take him left, to admin and comms.

He stopped just before the corner, listening. Someone was shouting from down there too. He glanced behind him; no one was coming out of the cafeteria—not yet. He stepped around the corner, swinging the rifle as he went so it pointed down the corridor.

Three men were coming his way. He didn't know them—probably from one of the outlier groups who'd just come into town. He mentally framed them as Tan Guy, Stumpy Guy, and Bared Teeth. Two of them had Glocks in their hands, Bared Teeth carried a tactical shotgun.

Vince flicked the AR-15 to full-auto. Stumpy Guy and Vince fired at the same moment, and Vince felt something burn a groove along the skin of his left shoulder as he fired a burst at the group. Stumpy Guy screamed and went down, clutching his belly, Tan Guy spun around, impacted hard in a shoulder. Bared Teeth was unhit; he had both hands on his gun and was carefully aiming.

Vince threw himself flat, firing another burst as he went down, and Bared Teeth lost his grimace, the bullets shattering his mouth and blowing out the back of his head. He writhed and fell flat on his back. Tan Guy got up to one knee and Vince fired a short burst, shooting him through the heart.

Vince stayed stretched out on his belly, waiting—and there was Marco Ambra, stepping out the door to the administration center, about forty feet away, aiming his Glock at Vince's face.

Vince fired, the rifle at an awkward angle, the burst tearing into Marco's right leg, knocking him off his feet. Marco fell face down, groaning, getting off a shot that zipped through the air above Vince.

Vince got quickly up on his elbows and fired, taking off the top of Marco's head before he could use the Glock again.

Marco flopped face-down, instantly dead.

Vince got to his feet, checked the load on the rifle—the clip was empty. He tossed the AR-15 aside and drew the Desert Eagle just in time to fire it at Bjorn, the strapping near-albino militiaman now running toward him with an Uzi.

The .50 round caught the guy in his gut, tearing him open and spinning him around. Bjorn fell heavily on his side, groaning.

But as Vince walked up to him, Bjorn raised the Uzi. Vince

kicked the weapon aside and shot Bjorn in the top of his head. At that range the big pistol made quite a mess.

He stepped over the body to the wall close to the open admin door. He stopped there, listening. No sound from within.

Vince looked around the edge of the door—saw no one down the hallway. Hearing voices from the stairway, at the second-floor level, he picked up the Uzi in his left hand, walked over to the stairwell and saw the shadows of men with guns coming up. He fired the Uzi randomly down the stairs, emptying the clip. A spray of bullets ricocheted below and the shadows receded. That would keep them for long enough, he figured.

He tossed the Uzi aside, went back to Marco's body, and found another set of keys on a chain attached to his belt. He broke it free. Vince holstered the Desert Eagle and picked up Bared Teeth's tactical shotgun—a Mossberg 500—and noticed that as well as a full magazine, it had five extra shells attached to the weapon's receiver by an elastic "side-saddle".

Shotgun in hand, he went to the door of the administrative offices. Standing to one side, he unlocked Gustafson's office door. He took hold of the knob, stepped to one side, pulling the door open wide. There was no response from inside. He stepped across the hallway, leaned over enough to see into the room. No one was there.

Vince went to the comm office, unlocked it the same way, opened the door the same way—also no response. He looked inside. No one there, just the electronics. PCs, printers, the tactical radio set up.

He thought about using the comms to try again to get in touch with the feds. Or maybe he could break into a computer and get some more data. But he was no hacker and didn't have time to try. The enemy would be coming up those stairs soon enough.

Let's get this done, he thought. Cut through the tango presence, find Deirdre and Bobby. The longer he waited, the more time the Brethren had to get their defense together.

Vince went to the corridor—and fired the tactical shotgun, instantly, shooting from the hip, at the four men at the top of the stairs just twenty feet away. The big gun bucked in his hands and one of the men exploded at the solar plexus. Vince pumped another round into the chamber as he brought the shotgun to his shoulder. A man behind the falling Brethren got off a shot that clipped Vince's right earlobe.

So much for getting my ear pierced someday, Vince thought, firing the Mossberg at the shooter. The man's face vanished in a welter of red as Vince stepped to his left, turning his body to make a smaller target as the guy with the Glock in his hand fired, the round going where Vince had been a moment before. The last man was farther down the stairs, seemed frozen with indecision.

Vince fired at the tango with the Glock, pumped the shotgun, and fired again. The four men lay still, sprawled half on top of one another, twitching in death. As he thumbed shells from the sidesaddle for reload, he recalled that he'd used a tactical shotgun in combat in one other fight, against a gang running guns to Boko Haram in Nigeria. Both times, it had been a handy weapon in close quarters.

He stepped carefully over the red-splashed, oozing bodies, ignoring the rank smell of shattered intestines, and went a few steps down, careful to watch the stairwell below. Blood splashed from the higher stairs; thin red waterfalls. As he went, Vince mentally reviewed the second floor: library, video center, conference room, extra storage. Nothing he needed to do here except fight his way through.

He got to the bottom, turned toward the door to the second floor—and a man stuck his plump, gaping face around the doorframe. Vince shot the NeoNazi in from about seven feet away. Blood and brains splashed and the man fell heavily to the floor.

Vince stopped, pumping the shotgun and listening. It was quiet, now, on the second floor. He hunkered down, grabbed the dead man by the back of the neck, and dragged him across the floor, the process making a big red smear on the concrete like something in a finger painting. He transferred the shotgun to his left hand, took hold of the dead man by the back of the belt, flipped his gurgling body around, and carried it close to the door, sticking the remains of the guy's head out into the hallway at waist level. An AR-15 rattled from the left and what remained of the corpse's head disintegrated. Vince dropped the body and waited, transferring the shotgun to his other hand.

"I think I got him!" someone yelled.

Vince stepped into the hallway and fired the shotgun at the man with the AR-15 near the library door. The militiaman screamed and staggered. He didn't catch the full load because he was about fifty feet away, so Vince took the shotgun into his left hand as with his right he pulled the Desert Eagle and fired, shooting the swaying militiaman through the heart. His target went down—and so did a second man running out of the library, Vince's shot cutting through his neck, the .50 round tearing away so much the head flopped over, held by a rag of skin and flesh, before the body dropped.

Vince turned to the right, firing the Desert Eagle instantly at another man stepping out of the video room doorway. The shot struck the NeoNazi in his right shoulder, the powerful impact spinning him around so that Vince's next round took him through the back.

Vince stepped back through the doorway to the stairwell. Softly singing "All Along the Watchtower", he reloaded the Desert Eagle and then the shotgun. He holstered the big pistol, stuck the barrel of the shotgun out into the hallway to see if it might make someone fire.

No response. He eased to the right against the wall by the door, peering down the hall to the left. He saw no one except the two dead men. He repeated the process on the other side of the door, looking right. Someone was ogling, down the hall—and Vince snapped a shot at him with the Mossberg. A chunk of doorframe vanished but he missed his target. The guy pulled back, yelling, "Oh shit!"

Vince turned, started down the stairs to the next floor. A startled man—Andy Kayson, his name was—stood on the next landing below with an AR-15 pointed at the floor. He was tanned, but for his perpetually red cheeks. His blond surfer-style hair was combed straight back, his neck decorated with Maori tattoos.

Kayson dropped the gun and raised his hands. "Don't shoot!"

"Hello, Andy," Vince said. "You just made what might be the first wise decision of your life. How many men down on the first floor?"

"Fuck, I don't know—maybe four or five. The General's got most of them organized out front. He thinks he's gonna get you when you come out. He's thinking of calling in the sheriff."

"So Woodbridge is in with you guys?"

"I guess. He's chummy with the General. What—what you going to do to me?"

"Depends on what you do now. You know the combination to the armory?"

"No—Wynn said it was something about 'Crystal Night' or something like that. Didn't hear nothing else."

"I see." *Kristallnacht*, Vince guessed. Named after broken glass from all the Jewish-owned stores when the Nazi pogrom was carried out on the nights of November ninth and tenth, in 1938. Was that the combination? *9101138?*

"Okay," Vince said. "Now drop the Glock too. Carefully."

Gingerly, Kayson took his Glock out of its holster and dropped the handgun on the stairs.

As Vince spoke to Kayson, part of his mind was listening for the sounds of Brethren on the floors above. There were a few still up there. So far, he heard no one coming. "Now head on down the stairs to the first floor, Andy. Slowly. Keep your hands up. Don't run, or I'll shoot you dead."

Licking his lips, Kayson turned around and started down the stairs.

As he followed, Vince paused long enough to pick up the Glock and stick it in his waistband. Then he joined Kayson at the bottom of the stairs. First floor, barracks, storage for food and medicine—and the armory. There was a separate stairway to the basement, down a short corridor.

"Now step on out, and yell at your friends not to shoot you!"

"I don't know, they... they're pretty nervous."

"Oh, come on, they're not stupid enough to shoot one of their Brethren. Go on, or I'll shoot you myself."

Kayson took two deep breaths, then yelled, "Don't shoot, it's me, Andy Kayson, I'm coming out!" He stepped out into the hallway—and looked to his left. "Wynn, don't shoot! I'm a prisoner!"

Vince stepped to the left side of the door and leaned over just enough to look right. He saw no one down that way. The stairs to the basement were down there, though.

"Andy, goddamnit, get outta the way!" Wynn Foster's voice.

"I can't—I gotta do what he says!"

"Good thinking," Vince said, transferring the shotgun to his left hand. He drew the Desert Eagle with his right, and then stepped out behind Kayson, firing past him with both weapons, the shotgun braced against his left hip, the pistol in his right hand. About forty feet away, Wynn Foster, assault rifle in hand, spun around and fell, his waist on the right side torn off by the shotgun blast as Vince fired three times at the three men behind Foster. The Brethren were wearing armored vests, so Vince aimed at their groins. Their combined screaming was ugly to hear as the big .50 rounds tore through their manhood and the base of their spines.

Andy Kayson shrieked in terror and ran out the open front door, which was partway between Vince and the men he'd killed —and Kayson was met by a hail of automatic weapons fire as the trigger-nervous Brethren out front reacted.

"Shit, that was one of ours," someone said hollowly.

Vince was already running to the right and through the open door to the separate stairway leading to the basement. He paused at the top, saw no one immediately below. He leaned the shotgun against the wall, reloaded the Desert Eagle and then began to descend the stairs…

CHAPTER FOURTEEN

"I'm gonna take you outta here and use your ass for bait!" That was Dale French's voice, coming from the basement corridor. "We got trouble upstairs and you're going to help!"

Vince stepped into the corridor and saw French about thirty-five feet off, standing by the open door to a cell.

Hanging from the door by her wrists—which were tied behind her—was Agent Deirdre Corlin, her face contorted in pain. French had his right hand on the doorknob, his left holding the keys he'd used to open it. He pocketed the keys and reached out to grab hold of her hair.

"You'd better kill me now or you'll be fucking sorry," she said between clenched teeth.

"That right?" French laughed. "I think there's time to teach you a lesson..."

Vince said, "Hello, French."

French looked up, startled, let go of the doorknob, put his hand on his holstered Glock.

Deirdre saw Vince and her eyes got big. "Kill him, Vince! Do it!"

"Glad to oblige a friend," Vince said, as French pulled his weapon.

Vince already had a bead on French's center-mass. He fired, and French was knocked off his feet by the force of the .50, skidding on his back, yelling in pain.

French struggled to a sitting position, raised the Glock, and Vince fired again, taking off the top of French's head from the bridge of his nose on up.

French's body flopped back and the Glock clacked on the floor.

Vince holstered the Desert Eagle, ran to Deirdre, unsheathing his knife. He cut the rope, catching Deirdre in the crook of his left arm to lower her to the floor, and then he cut the knot around her wrists. She groaned as he cut through the plastic ties.

"Oh god," she said, tears of relief flowing as she put her hands in front of her. "That hurts too... but what a relief... But... ow." She leaned over, rocking in place from the pain. "Oh fuck."

"Are your arms dislocated?" he asked.

"I don't think so." She grimaced, moving her shoulders around. "Some swelling. I think I can use them."

"I brought you a gun, if you can hold it."

"I'd love a gun, thank you very much. I can deal with it."

"Let me lift you up, till we know for sure about your shoulders..." He gripped her just under her ribcage and lifted her to her feet, then stepped back from her.

"Oh... hurts like a bitch." She shifted her shoulders again. "They seem in place—but *so* fucking sore."

He held out the Glock, butt first. "You sure you can handle that right now?"

"Yes..." She took the handgun and hefted it. "Oh yes indeed."

"Who's out there?" shouted a voice from the other cell.

Vince stepped over to the other cell door. Bobby Destry looked through the barred window at Vince. "Vince Bellator?"

"That's right. Hold on, I'll get you out of there."

"Bellator!" someone shouted from up the top of the stairs. "You come out with your hands up, we'll take you into custody alive!"

It was Gustafson's voice, remote, hard to hear. He was shouting from near the front door.

"I'll think about it!" Vince shouted. "Give me five minutes!"

Vince went to French's body, muttering, "Robbing a lot of corpses today..." as he took the keys from the dead man's pants pocket.

He returned to Bobby's cell, unlocked it, and the young man stepped out. "Oh shit, dude! Is this a dream?"

"Nope," Vince said, clapping him on the shoulder. "More of a real messy reality." He grinned at Bobby. "Your mom sent me!"

"That's embarrassing!" Bobby laughed. "But I'm gonna kiss her, first thing when I see her."

"First things first. You willing to shoot any of your ex compadres if you have to?"

"If I have to. Except Shaun. I don't think I could shoot him." He looked past Vince at the bloody remains of French. "Um— Shaun's still *alive*...isn't he?"

"Last I saw of him." Vince turned to Deirdre who was rubbing her shoulders with her hands. "You okay to move out?"

"More than ready." She looked at Bobby. "Good to see you in person."

"You guys were talking cell to cell?" Vince asked.

"Before they hung me up." She checked the gun over, nodded to herself, and said, "You send that email for me?"

"I did. No response last time I checked. I tried to get in touch with the FBI on the phone. Couldn't get anyone to really listen. Just receptionists and voicemail."

"Gustafson says he's got people in the Justice Department…"

"Yeah, I figured. Also he's pally with Sheriff Woodbridge."

"How are we getting out of here?"

"First we're stopping at the armory. See if I can get it open. Then… we're going up to the heli."

"How'd you get into the base? They've been watching for you."

"I climbed up the east side and took out the emplacements. We should head up to the heli. You think you can still pilot a chopper—even with your arms swollen?"

"I think so." She was pale, her face taut from the pain in her shoulders. But she seemed grimly determined.

Vince nodded and said, "Bobby—pistol or shotgun?"

"I'm not that good a shot."

"Shotgun it is. Come on. Everyone stay quiet as possible."

Vince led the way to the stairs, leaned through the stairwell door just enough to look up, and saw no one up above. They started slowly up the stairs. He got to the first-floor landing, paused, looked both ways down the hall. Still no one.

"Bellator!" This time Gustafson's voice was louder, coming through a bullhorn. "Come on out! We're not waiting any longer!"

Vince turned to the others and said in a low voice, "Bobby—you take that shotgun against the wall there. Deirdre—I was told the armory combination is something to do with *Kristallnacht*. That sound right to you?"

"I haven't heard hint-one about the code for that door. Nothing."

"Okay—if you two can watch the front door, and just discourage anyone trying to come in, I'm going to try to get into that armory. I've got some thoughts about covering our exfil."

Deirdre nodded. There was a dark glitter in her eyes.

I wouldn't like to be the Brethren who tries to cross her now, Vince thought.

He watched them move close enough to the door that they could see out. Then he sprinted past the doorway and back through the open space under the airshaft, toward the reinforced steel door of the armory. Someone fired through the front door at him. Then he was at the armory door, which was out of the line of fire from the front. He heard the boom of a shotgun and the crack of the Glock as Bobby and Deirdre engaged in suppressive fire to keep the Brethren from coming through the front door.

He tried the dates of *Kristallnacht* on the door's entry keyboard. He tapped in:

9101138

A little red light came on under the keyboard. Wrong passkey. A spate of gunshots came through the front door, cracking into the concrete to his left. One of them ricocheted close by.

Vince tried the first day of *Kristallnacht* only, along with the month and year. He tapped in:

91138

The little light turned green and the door clicked ajar. A light switched on inside.

He grinned, swung the heavy steel door wide and rushed into the armory. The room was like an extra-large bank vault, but instead of money, the racks and shelves on the walls were chocka-block with ordnance. There were several light machine guns, four FN-SCAR rifles, two old-school collector's item Tommy guns with the drums on them, a rack of Mossberg 500 tactical shotguns, a row of Uzis, and several boxes of grenades, including flashbangs. On the opposite wall was a rack of AK47s and another of AR-15s. On the floor below them was a mortar with a box of shells and… an RPG launcher with four rocket grenades.

There were also rows of green-steel ammo boxes.

The ATF would have a field day in here, he thought.

Vince selected two frag grenades, two flashbangs, a loaded Tommy gun—and the RPG launcher.

He heard another exchange of gunfire out front and wondered if he had made the right tactical choices. Suppose after all she'd been through, Deirdre got killed there on the first floor? Maybe they should have run for the heli first thing. But Vince wanted to drive the militia back as far as possible from the base before taking the heli. He put the hand grenades and flashbangs in his pockets, carried the launcher out under one arm, the Tommy gun under the other, set them against the inner wall of the airshaft, just out of line of sight of the Brethren, and ran back for the rocket grenades. He ran into the armory and scooped the rocket grenades up in both arms.

Keeping under cover of the out-jutting wall of the air shaft, Vince returned to the launcher, bullets screaming past the wall on his right, to smack into the concrete beside the door of the armory. He crouched to load the RPG, then stood up, yelled, "Deirdre, Bobby—what's your sitrep?"

"We're okay," she shouted. "They're staying back."

"Pull back to the stairs to the roof!"

"Copy that!"

He heard them moving back, then he stepped out into the open, aimed the RPG launcher through the open doorway toward the small guard tower on the inner wall of the compound, and fired.

The rocket grenade made a *whumpf* and hissed on its way as Vince stepped back. Though he'd been exposed for only a second, a fusillade of shots smacked into the back wall of the airshaft—then there was a *thud* of RPG impact, bringing the clattering of metal fragments from the guard tower; shrapnel striking vehicles and outbuildings... and at least one man. Someone screamed piteously.

Vince scooped up the Tommy gun, exposed his right side just enough to fire it from his hip, and sprayed the entire drum of .45 rounds at the courtyard of the compound, toward every spot where a man could be taking cover.

Someone cursed. Glass shattered; metal resounded with bullet impacts.

He stepped back, getting a glimpse of muzzle flashes to the north of one of the outbuildings. He tossed the empty Tommy gun aside, loaded another rocket grenade into the RPG and stepped out to fire it at the muzzle flashes.

Someone shouted, "RPG!"

The grenade whooshed, then it struck the corner of the steel building near a group of shooters. A man shrieked, and another, as more shrapnel zinged through the compound.

Vince loaded another RPG round, then heard a truck engine revving. He glanced around the edge of the wall at the compound to see a big four-wheel-drive pickup roaring right at him. Several Brethren were standing in the back, firing Glocks.

He swung the RPG out, braced; bullets sizzled past his head as he fired. He stepped quickly back undercover without seeing the rocket strike home.

But the rocket grenade struck the truck in the center of its grill, stopping it about fifty feet away. When he looked again, he saw an expanding ball of fire, and pieces of truck and humanity flying. Smoke and chaos from the exploded, crumpled truck, so close to the doorway, gave Vince the cover he had hoped for. He reloaded the RPG then bolted from his position, running to the stairs.

"Come on!" he shouted at Deirdre and Bobby. Carrying the launcher, he started up the stairs. They came after him, and the three of them ran up the metal stairway, flight after flight.

But partway they had to slow at bodies Vince had left, blood still pattering down the stairs, so they could step over the corpses, and parts of corpses.

Deirdre glanced down a hallway at the next floor and said, "More of 'em! How many you kill, Vince? Jesus!"

"Let's keep moving!" he said, leading the way.

They kept on, gasping for air by the time they reached the top floor of the bunker complex.

"Up this ladder," Vince said, breathing hard. "Oh, wait— Deirdre, can you climb with your arms all kind of…"

"Yeah, I can climb. It'll hurt. But so what." She started up the ladder, grimacing with pain, and climbed through the trap door.

Vince heard shouts from the stairway below. Unintelligible but urgent. "Go on, Bobby."

Bobby Destry put the shotgun's strap over his shoulder, climbed up and through.

"Pull the RPG up after you!" Vince called. He handed the loaded launcher up through the trap door and then looked down the stairwell and saw a flight and a half down. A bullet cracked up the stairwell and hit the concrete ceiling above Vince. He stepped back, selected a frag grenade from his pockets, pulled the pin and tossed it down the stairs. Men shouted and ran back down.

He returned to the ladder and stared up, hearing the explosion and the metallic clattering of grenade shrapnel from the stairs.

Suppose the heli isn't fueled up? Vince wondered as he climbed through the hatch, locking it down behind him. But it had to be fueled with Operation Firepower about to happen. Didn't it?

"Help me uncover the helicopter, Bobby," Vince said. "Bring that RPG, leave it by the heli door." The three of them ran to the heli.

As Vince unsheathed his knife, he could hear more shouting from down in the compound and a distorted voice on a bullhorn. *"Surrender… we will… forced…"*

Vince smiled. They had no notion he was taking the helicopter.

He cut the lines holding the camouflage netting and they pulled it off the rotors and fuselage. The rotors were folded down, so nothing got caught, and the heli was soon free. Deirdre climbed the metal roll-up stairs to the hatch. "The damn thing is locked," she said.

Vince went up the short flight of steps to the hatch beside her and dug in his pockets. "Hold on, maybe one of these keys…" He tried Marco's keys—the third one opened the hatch. "I think the other one here'll start it…" He handed her the keys, tugged the hatch out of the way, and Deirdre went in—stopping just inside the door to stare at the big M134 minigun. It was pulled back on a rail welded into the deck, and locked in place. "What the hell!"

"Yeah," Vince said. "They had some plans for that thing. Better get us in the air."

She went to the pilot's seat and put on the helmet with its headset and earphones. Bobby took a seat beside her as Vince brought the RPG in.

The engine roared to life. "How's the fuel?" Vince called.

"Full tank!" Deirdre said, unlocking the rotors.

The rotor blades unfolded and turned, faster and faster, whipping around, raising dust around the heli. Vince remained standing beside the open hatch; he held the loaded RPG in one hand, holding onto a stanchion with the other.

The heli lifted up, a little crookedly, but about fifty feet up.

"Corlin! Take it out over the emplacements and soon as I fire, head east!"

She veered the chopper out over the near edge of the compound where Vince could see a group of men just outside the gate standing by an SUV. Beyond them, a Humvee was driving away from the compound. It was out of range. But firing downward, he had a pretty good chance of hitting that SUV.

He triggered the RPG launcher, there came the *whumpf* and hiss, and the rocket grenade sped down, straight for the SUV. He could see men running—and then the rocket struck the vehicle in the center of its roof. It was hidden by the explosion.

Deirdre was already accelerating to the east and angling up. Vince tossed the RPG out the door, reached out—with a good grip on the stanchion—and pulled the hatch shut. He went to a seat, buckling in behind Deirdre.

"Where are we headed?" she asked.

"Head northeast for Stonewall, Agent Corlin, and kill the heli's lights. Bobby—we're going to need directions…"

Rose Destry lived on the outskirts of Stonewall, in the countryside to the east. There was a big, empty field behind her house that she had rented out to farmers in earlier times. Now it was overgrown with knee-high grass and weeds.

Gustafson's helicopter settled down in the field, as close to the house as Deirdre dared.

"Switch on the lights!" Vince yelled.

The heli's lights came on; a few seconds later, so did the lights over the back deck of the house about fifty yards away.

Watching through the window, Vince could see Rose Destry, in a nightgown, coming out on the back porch.

"Bobby—go on home and take care of your Mom!" Vince said.

Bobby came over to him and, over the rumble of the idling engine and the whine of the slowly whirling rotors, he said, "I got to thank you, man. You saved my life. I know it. They were never going to let me live." He put out his hand and Vince shook it.

"Go on, bro—and listen: Take your mom out of Stonewall for a while. Just talk her into it. Leave before dawn. Get out of town and, I don't know, visit Florida or someplace. Get out of state. Be safer."

Bobby nodded. "Yeah. We'll do it." He turned to Deirdre and said, "Thanks for the ride, ma'am!"

She looked over her shoulder—wincing at the pain this brought—and managed a smile.

Then Bobby opened the hatch, jumped down and ran toward his mother.

Vince watched, smiling, as Chris's little brother ran to Rose Destry and into her arms.

"Take us up, Agent Corlin!" he called, shutting the hatch. "And lights out!"

The rotors whirled faster, the engine hum deepened, and the heli rose into the sky.

She slanted up to three-thousand feet and leveled off, heading northwest toward Washington D.C. When they got in close enough to the nation's capital, they'd have to switch the lights on to avoid looking suspicious.

Would Gustafson report the heli stolen? Maybe. Or maybe "the General" wouldn't want the attention that would bring.

They flew onward toward the D.C. area, and Vince felt himself getting sleepy—when he'd been in the Rangers and Delta Force, he'd had to catnap on flights between missions, and he still had a tendency to go to sleep on a flight. Climbing the cliff and the intense action afterwards was hard work...

He heard Deirdre call out that she was going to reduce elevation near a cell tower so she could call Agent Chang. Vince nodded and slipped into sleep, almost immediately dreaming.

Chris was walking beside him through the Yucatan jungle, both of them in cammies, guns in hand, on mission. Tropical sunlight speared down through the trees. "You sure this is the life you want, Vince?" Chris asked.

"It's all I'm good for," Vince said. "Too damaged for anything else, man."

"You can heal."

"*You* can't. You're dead. I'm going to find the pricks who did it. Bosses didn't want me to follow up on that mission. I had to walk away. But Angel Lopez is still out there, Chris. I'm gonna find the son of a bitch. I had to do this first—bury your hand, see your mom. Help your brother. Now I've got to finish it with the asshole who killed you. The asshole who kills people with heroin and meth every damn day..."

"It's not all up to you, Vince..."

"No one else is taking Lopez down."

Chris seemed suddenly taller than Vince. Till he realized that Chris was now floating a foot off the ground. He was still marching along, but in the air. Now he was three feet off the ground. Now he was floating upward and vanishing in the tree cover...

"Chris—where you going, brother?" Vince called, peering up through the trees.

"There's got to be a better life for you out there, Vince," came Chris's voice from the air.

"It's too late for me! You know how many men I killed today? I'm going to be on the run... May as well do some good while I'm out there..."

"You don't have to do this, Vince..."

"Vince!" It was Deirdre's voice, shouting from the front of the heli.

He opened his eyes, sat up, and looked around. The jungle was still there—but fading now. And gone. He was in the helicopter heading for D.C.

"Whoa, fell asleep..." He got up and went to sit beside her. "What's up?"

"I called Agent Chang. I got through this time. But he's in hiding. The Attorney General seems to be targeting him and me both!"

Vince snorted. "The AG? Dawson? I've heard stories about that guy. I didn't think he was this deep into it..."

"Richie found some connections between him and Gustafson."

"Richie?"

"Agent Chang. Whom you're going to meet in about half an hour."

"Where? We can't just land at any airport in a stolen heli..."

"There's a small airport south of town. Anyway, it used to be

179

an airport. It's just a lot of weedy concrete now, I guess. It's in an industrial district and there's no one around out there tonight. He's going to meet us there."

"You sure we can trust this guy?"

"Richie? Absolutely. I've known him since the academy. Worked closely with him on two seriously fucked-up assignments. That's where you get to know if you can trust a guy."

Vince nodded. "Yes, it is."

"I'm trying to decide who I should radio about the attack tomorrow. Let them know there's a domestic terrorism strike. Chang says I'm *persona non grata* in the Bureau right now. There's some guy named Aaron Stigler—new administrator in the Georgia FBI offices. The guy's been slandering me, calling me a paranoid drug addict!"

"What!"

"Yeah and I don't even smoke pot. And he's never met me! The guy has to be with the Brethren. So between him and Dawson I don't know who I can trust at the Bureau right now. I could call the D.C. police…"

"Got to," Vince said, nodding. "There's risks in doing that, but it's got to be done. Call the D.C. cops and tell them what's going to happen at the Lincoln Memorial tomorrow."

"Suppose you've discouraged Gustafson to the point where he's called the attack off?"

"Let's hope so. But I doubt it."

"Yeah, Gustafson made a point of being able to make it happen no matter what. And he's organized it in a way that he can seem to be detached from the whole thing. They can commit mass murder—and it can seem like he had nothing to do with it…"

Shaun Adler sat nervously in the chair in Mr. Ostrovsky's house in the mountains of West Virginia, waiting for them to bring him the suicide vest. It was well after midnight, and the wind was rattling the wooden shutters over the windows.

He looked at the window, wondering if he could escape that way. It looked like it was painted shut. Could he smash the glass and escape? But there were sentries around the house.

He had watched the route nervously as they drove up into the mountains of West Virginia. He wanted to know where he was so he could find his way to help—if he could slip away from the house.

They'd caught him walking up the road, away from Wolf Base. He'd been heading for the highway, the night before, planning to duck into the bushes, and then the Humvee rolled up, and he heard the General's voice. "Mac, get that deserter in this vehicle. See that he's disarmed."

Colls had directed him at gunpoint to get in the back of the Humvee between him and Buster Sedge. Buster, a heavy-set man with a thick, curly black beard, had been one of Gustafson's students before the General had been kicked out of the university. Buster was the one to say it first, as they drove toward the highway. "Maybe he can be the one to wear the vest since we've lost the other guy…"

Now he sat waiting in a chilly little bedroom in the back of the enormous gray-stone house. It smelled of mildew; there was a painting on the wall so faded he couldn't make out what the image was. Gustafson referred to the big country house as his "Black Forest retreat".

Gustafson was here somewhere, upstairs, monitoring the set-up for Operation Firepower. Shaun had heard enough discussion in the Humvee to guess that Firepower would be happening in D.C. And he was to be a decoy for it.

Greeting them at the door, Pieter Ostrovsky, a cadaverous old Russian in a fine Italian suit, had said, "Gentlemen, welcome to the most comfortable safe-house in North America…" Along with Colls and Buster, there were six Brethren from the West Virginia chapter here, too, as protection for Gustafson.

Now Shaun heard footsteps creaking in the hall, and the door opened. Mac Colls came in with Polly Sulevich. She was a Shield Maiden, about forty years old, for a West Virginia chapter of the Brethren.

Polly had some straight pins pinched in her lips, and the vest, without the explosives in it, draped over a forearm. In her other hand was a little sewing bag. She was a chipmunk-cheeked little woman with bright red lipstick and flaxen hair up in a bun on her head. The suicide vest was khaki colored, had started life as an ammunition vest for hunters.

They'd assured Shaun that it wouldn't have real explosives in it when the time came. But he knew they were lying. Because they'd reassured him too many times. And because he'd stopped trusting them anyway. He had seen Gustafson's willingness to throw away the lives of his men.

"Stand up and put your arms up for the measurement," Colls said gruffly.

Shaun did as he was told. "I wasn't deserting, Sarge," Shaun said, hoping he was lying convincingly. "I was just taking a breather… saw a couple of friends of mine blown up by that RPG round and I just…"

"You sure as fuck were deserting," Colls said. "Now shut up and cooperate so you can make up for it."

He stood up, and Colls went to sit on the bed and opened a cell phone.

God if I could get hold of a cell phone, Shaun thought, as he went to Polly down by the dresser. He knew Vince's phone number...

"Canville? Colls," Mac said, talking on the phone. "Is everyone in place in Alexandria? Yeah? And so what?"

Polly spoke to Shaun chirpily as she fitted him for the suicide vest. "You are such a brave young man," she said in her thick Ukrainian accent. "To go to pull the wool over the police, yes? I admire you so much! Stand still please... we must make this tight to you, so it does not stand out so much under your jacket... Now—turn around...

Shaun turned around and just stood there, arms up, as she tugged the vest closer around him, and he wondered if Vince Bellator was still alive. It didn't seem likely.

There was a small dresser in front of him, and on it was the little sewing bag. And in the sewing were little spindles and needles and a pack of cigarettes with a lighter stuck in its cellophane and... a cell phone. He stared at the phone. Then looked quickly away.

He could hear Mac talking on the other phone. "Yes... well, you'll get your briefing. You know the drill: stand down but stand by..."

Mac was sitting on the bed, talking—didn't sound like he was looking Shaun's way.

Shaun looked at the phone in the sewing bag. She'd probably notice if he took it.

But what if she didn't? There was a lot of junk in that bag.

"Suck in your belly, my brave boy!" Polly said. "I must get this tight!"

He pretended to do just that—but only did it a little so she'd have to struggle with the vest. She muttered in Ukrainian as she jerked the belt tighter—and he used her distraction to reach out, grab the phone, and push it up under his vest in front.

"Now then, that is good!" Polly said, buckling something he couldn't see.

Shaun pretended to stretch a little and managed to flip the sewing mostly shut so she wouldn't see into it when she picked it up.

"You got that thing adjusted yet, Polly?" Mac asked.

"Almost… I must be careful not to… well… almost done…"

Shaun thought, The suicide vest—is live.

CHAPTER FIFTEEN

Vince had found some cold-press coffee in the big heli's minifridge, and he was drinking it from the bottle as he walked out onto the cracked old runway. Deirdre Corlin was just coming down the extending steps from the helicopter cab.

The moon was sinking toward the horizon, looking big and yellow over the almost featureless buildings of the industrial park. Rotors slowing almost to a stop, the helicopter was sitting in the middle of the abandoned runway, about two hundred yards from the little, boarded-over control tower. It had been a small airport for private planes, once; now it was mostly a canvas for graffiti artists.

Deirdre walked up beside him and said, "I see you finally cleaned the mud off your face and hands. It's an improvement."

"Oh, thanks. I learned to wash when I was a boy. Sometimes I remember."

She smiled, and he liked that he'd made her smile.

Seeing headlights swivel onto the edge of the big concrete apron, Vince stopped where he was and shifted the coffee into his left hand, putting his right on the butt of his gun.

"Is that him?" Vince asked as Deirdre stepped up beside him.

"If it isn't, we're screwed," she said, calmly.

"Good to know."

The black Crown Vic pulled up to their left, and the engine shut off, but the driver left the headlights on.

An Asian-American guy got out. He was about thirty-five, wearing a gray-blue suit, black tie, white shirt. Classic FBI, Vince thought.

"Hey, Corlin," he said. But he was eyeing Vince.

"Hey, Richie. This is Vince Bellator."

Agent Chang walked up to Vince and they shook hands. Vince was a head taller than Chang, probably had fifty pounds on him too. But he seemed a wiry, confident man. "Mr. Bellator." He looked past them at the heli. "You've got your own helicopter, now, Corlin?"

"Sure," she said. "Weren't you issued one?"

"We kind of borrowed it," Vince said. "But the guy we borrowed it from was trying to kill us."

"Is that a *machine gun* inside there?" he asked, staring at it.

"Ah—it is," Vince said. "Yeah. Gustafson had that put in. He didn't get to use it."

"So that's a stolen helicopter…"

Deirdre shrugged. "Technically."

Chang let out a long breath and shook his head. "You didn't go right to the nearest Bureau office and just… I don't know… turn it in?"

"You can't land a huge helicopter like that just anywhere," she said.

"Anyway, we had to get here *fast*," Vince said. "Agent Corlin told you what's going down tomorrow morning?"

Chang grimaced. "Yeah, Corlin told me. If they go through with it. I was trying to get the Bureau on board but... they're calling me in. They want me to turn in my gun and badge, for now. Pending investigation. Just like Corlin here."

Deirdre shook her head in disgust. "The idiots! I called it in to the D.C. police, Richie—and soon as they heard my name, they said I was wanted for questioning and they discounted the whole report! They said there are *dozens* of calls about an attack, and some say it's this place and some say that place and they've decided they're all bogus, some kind of 'fringe group harassment'."

"That's Gustafson's work," Vince said. "Disinformation is a standard white supremacist tactic. Dozens of false tips to cover up the real attack." He looked at Chang. "There have to be FBI agents who're willing to listen."

He nodded. "There are. Thing is, Director Dawson is under investigation himself, by an inspector general. He's under a lot of suspicion. Justice Department's in turmoil. Lots of agents don't trust him. But they don't want to go against orders, either. They could lose their job—their pensions."

"We need to get what help we can and stop this thing."

"You're sure it's *on*...?" Chang asked. "Corlin told me what happened at the base..."

Vince said, "I believe it is. Gustafson has been preparing for the attack for more than two years. And we can't take a chance. A lot of innocent lives are on the line."

Chang said, "I hear that." He cocked his head to one side and looked at Vince appraisingly. "But... really, I should arrest you. Stolen chopper. Piles of bodies at Wolf Base. Interstate flight. Maybe you had good reasons, but—that doesn't make it legal."

"Can't let you arrest me," said Vince in an apologetic tone. "But I can promise not to hurt you much if you try."

Chang blinked and his head rocked back a little. "You're kind of over-confident, aren't you?"

"Do we need a pissing contest now?" Deirdre growled. "Richie, he could take you down before you touched your gun. Just trust me. I've read his files. And I've seen him in action. He's a highly decorated Delta Force specialist."

Chang cleared his throat. "Just asking. So... now what?"

"You have to try to get law enforcement on this," Vince said. "And I have to be there in case it doesn't. Meanwhile—is there a place in the area has breakfast twenty-four hours?"

I don't see how you can eat at a time like this," Deirdre said, shaking her head as Vince ate his second plate of eggs and hash browns. Chang—not wanting to know too much about Vince's plans—had dropped them off here. They were in a back corner booth of a Denny's, almost the only customers. Willie Nelson sang "Crazy" from the sound system. He sounded lost in the nearly empty restaurant.

"Need to eat at a time like this," Vince said, refilling his cup from the carafe. "Going to need the energy. I'll burn through it all before the day's over..."

"Or we'll just sit twiddling our fingers." Deirdre had ordered orange juice. She took a sip of it, made a face, and said, "I don't see what we can do—we could've been misled about their target."

"I don't think so," Vince said. He drank some coffee and added, "Anyway, I can't ask you to go with me and do what I'm going to do. You can do it if you choose to—but I can't ask it of you."

188

"Which is what?"

"There's plan A and plan B. Plan A, I would need you to fly the heli. That's probably what would work best. But it'd ruin your career—more than this bullshit smear going on right now. So I guess Plan B... I show up on foot and do what I can. Maybe you and Richie can help me on the ground."

Deirdre crossed her arms and rubbed her shoulders. "I'm going to stop Gustafson no matter what it takes. Career or not."

"How's the pain in your shoulders?"

"Hurts. There's some swelling. But the ibuprofen helped. I've made up my mind I'm going to fly that heli..."

The phone in Vince's pack rang. The small pack was on the seat beside him, and he opened it, putting the phone to his ear. "Yeah?"

He half expected to hear a threat from Gustafson. But it was Shaun Adler's voice, whispering, "Can you hear me okay? I can't raise my voice..."

"I can hear you. You at Wolf Base?"

"No. West Virginia. Place called Ostrovsky House, big stone place right at the end of Greenville Road, a little south of a town called Wersted in the Adirondacks. They're holding me here, Vince—they're making me put on a suicide vest."

Vince felt a sick chill go through him. He had bad memories of suicide bombers. And *forced* suicide bombers were something he'd seen too; a monstrous terrorist practice carried out more than once by ISIS.

"Do you know where they're going to deploy you?"

"Police precinct. Third district, and I heard the number three-oh-five. But I'm not sure. Maybe a cop shop, man. I just know it's happening not long before the attack, around nine and—*shit!*"

"Shaun?"

Vince heard Mac Colls' voice then, in the background. *"Who are you talking to, Adler? What are you doing with that phone?"*

"It's my dad, I just wanted him to know I'm okay—"

Then the connection cut off.

Vince slapped the phone down on the table. "That was Shaun Adler. I am very much afraid I'm not going to be able to help him…"

"Anything about the Brethren's plan?"

"There was one thing—third district, three-oh-five… You know what, I need you to call Agent Chang…"

The Uber driver had been surprised when they asked him to let them off at the edge of the old airport. But he didn't seem to have reported it to anyone, because Vince and Deirdre Corlin had been here for hours.

Deirdre was stretched out on the deck of the helicopter, dozing with her head on her arms; Vince was in the co-pilot's chair. The horizon to the east, between buildings, was glowing gray-red in pre-dawn. He glanced back at Deirdre; saw she was in a fitful sleep, her eyes opening then fluttering shut.

He had thought about flying to West Virginia. Thinking if he could capture Gustafson, he could force him to stop the attack. And rescue Shaun at the same time.

But he suspected the whole thing was autonomous by now. The attack would go ahead. And Gustafson might well not surrender peacefully, anyway.

Right now, Vince was considering calling an old friend who worked at the Pentagon. Major Gus Gresley. Gus was now the Delta Force officer at the Pentagon, with an office in the

DIA. There was some risk in a call like that. Maybe Gresley had heard that Vince had "gone rogue". With Dawson in the Justice Department, and connections between Dawson and Gustafson, there was a good chance of it. Question was, would Gresley believe Vince—or the rumors?

Vince shrugged. Worth a try. He got out his phone. He remembered numbers, always had. And he remembered Gresley's home phone number.

After four rings, Gresley answered, his voice thick. "Who the hell?"

"It's Vince Bellator, is who the hell. Sorry to wake you, Gus, but I ran into some guys who plan to attack the Joint Chiefs tomorrow. They want to kill them all. There's a meeting with the generals and the DIA—that right?"

"How'd you know about the meeting?"

"A certain Professor Gustafson. Who has friends on the inside at the Justice Department and the Pentagon. He's a Nazi asshole, Gus. It's the Germanic Brethren. They're planning a group of attacks, including the Joint Chiefs. Tomorrow, sometime before nine…"

"A *group* of attacks?"

"Yeah. Me and… my associate here… we've tried to tell the Bureau and the D.C. police but we're getting no headway. Same with Homeland Security. They told us to call the FBI who told us to call Homeland Security… The Attorney General has poisoned the waters. My understanding is, the main attack is at nine-thirty at the Lincoln Memorial—a hundred twenty domestic terrorists in six trucks."

"There's a big Democratic Party event happening there… though Lincoln was a Republican… but then the Republican Party was more like…"

"You still half asleep, Gus?"

"Yeah, and confused. I took a sleeping pill. And how am I supposed to act on this? You're classed as a criminal; they've got you pegged as a lone nut killer or something. That's what I hear. Something about a lot of dead guys in Georgia."

"They were Germanic Brethren and they were trying to kill me. Anyway, you don't have to give me as the source. Maybe the city cops will take the intel seriously if it comes from you. They need to cancel that event. And you need to cancel the other one. The Joint Chiefs. Be ready to take down a lone gunman coming to the site of the meeting…"

"We've been getting warnings about attacks all day. One was going to be on the Capitol Building, one was on the White House, one was at Georgetown U. Just a lot of crazy contradictory stuff. I don't think anyone's going to listen to you or me."

"Me, no. Your credibility is still good, though, Gus."

"Not in a way that gets fast action. This big Democratic Party event at the Lincoln Memorial has been planned for a long time, and the theory is, far-right-nutters are trying to get them to cancel it with a hoax about an attack. No one's inclined to listen."

"Did I not once save your life?"

"Yes."

"Have I always been a guy you could trust, or not?"

"You have been. I believe you, Vince. But—"

"Do what you can. And better drink some coffee. You don't want to go back to sleep tonight, Gus."

Vince hung up, and wondered if he should call Homeland Security again…

192

But it didn't seem like anyone was going to listen to him. Which left just one option.

Dawn in West Virginia. "Will he get there on time?" Buster asked.

Mac nodded. "Oh yeah. If they leave now."

They were in the garage of the Ostrovsky house, loading weapons into the trunk of Mac's old Buick LeSabre.

Buster tucked the Uzi, in its canvas bag, in a corner by the AR-15 and the cooler with the food and coffee for the trip. "Adler going to have that vest on when he's in the car with us?"

"You think I'm crazy? No. It's in the trunk of the car that dumbass Flesky is driving all by his lonesome. So if it goes off…" He shook his head. "Not with me in the car! I want to die fighting for the cause, not because of some stupid fucking mistake."

"Flesky on his way there?" Buster asked.

"Yeah, he left an hour ago. He'll be waiting near the building where they're having the meeting. We'll get the vest on the kid, and Flesky will drive him to the precinct. You follow in this car, while I take care of the Joint Chiefs. Then you head to the memorial."

"Sounds good." Buster closed the trunk. "You've got some balls, taking that Joint Chiefs mission, Mac."

"Got to. Fucking Bellator was a big disappointment, a fraud just like I said. I warned the General…"

"Bellator lied about everything, yeah. But he's pretty fucking effective. Killed a lot of good Brethren."

"He'll suffer for what he did. We'll find whoever he cares about and make them all suffer for it. Now let's get the kid. It's dawn. We've got to hit the road. Three hours to get to D.C."

"Traffic should be light from here," Buster said, following Mac out of the garage.

They went through the kitchen to the hall, up the stairs, down another hall to the room where Shaun Adler waited. Mac unlocked the door—and found Shaun standing at the window, staring out. Like he was thinking about getting away, Mac thought.

"Forget it, Adler," Mac said. "You're all done deserting. Come on—we're hitting the road!"

He hooked a thumb toward the door and stepped out of the way. Looking pale and scared, Shaun Adler walked past him and Buster to the hallway. "Go left and down the stairs. We're going to the garage."

"Can I talk to the General, first?" Shaun asked at the top of the stairs.

"Nope. No one trusts you after you made that hinky phone call. You just do what you're told and it'll all be alright."

Shaun nodded—then he rushed down the stairs and turned toward the front door.

"He's trying to rabbit!" Buster said.

"No shit," Mac muttered, hurrying down the stairs.

He caught up with Shaun at the front door where he was just turning the knob. Mac grabbed him by the belt and the neck, wrenched him away from the door, and slammed him into the wall. The blow smacked Shaun's forehead into the dark wooden panel—and he went limp, slipping down to sag onto his knees.

Mac examined Shaun as Buster caught up, puffing. "He dead?"

"No, out cold. He'll be alright. Let's carry him out to the Buick. When he comes to, you keep your gun on him. Keep it down below the windows, but make sure he doesn't try to get away again… The

General has every element in place and this little fuck is not going to ruin it for us. Our destiny is to see this all the way through."

Buster nodded. "This is our *Schicksal.*"

Vince was peering at the GPS on his phone, examining, for the tenth time, the terrain and streets around the Lincoln Memorial.

He went over it again in his mind and just didn't see any other way. Not with so many trucks coming at the Brethren's target—and coming from six places.

He heard Deirdre moaning in her sleep, and he swiveled the seat to see her twitching, her fingers clenching.

She gasped and sat bolt upright, staring wildly around. Her hair was mussed, and she was panting softly. "Oh Jesus. I thought I was…"

"You were back in that cell?" Vince asked softly.

"Yes." She brushed hair out of her eyes. "Fuck this. There any more coffee?"

"In the fridge."

She got up, wincing at the pain in her shoulders and back, and went stiffly to the minifridge, getting herself a bottle of cold coffee.

"I was captured, in Syria," he said. "They tortured me. Mostly with electricity. Car batteries. Beatings. They treated me to a waterboarding, too, because, they said, the CIA was doing it."

"It was." She opened the coffee and drank a little. "I saw in your file you were captured and tortured. Command advised you not to go back in-country for at least three months. Maybe transfer to the states, work as a trainer. You talked them into letting you stay on the job."

"I had to wait till I could get a mission in that town. Where I could slip off, after, and take care of those assholes. That way…"

"Catharsis."

He nodded. "Pretty much." He gave a dry chuckle. "Helped a little."

"How'd you get away? It didn't say. Just that you escaped."

"Someone was careless. They tied my hands in front of me and turned their back." He shrugged. "I killed him and four others and headed out."

"When you went back…"

"Only three of them left from… before. But I took care of them. Just—cut their throats."

"You didn't torture them."

"No one should torture anyone. Not them, not us."

"I agree."

"Did it take a long time to get past it?"

"I… would like to tell you I got completely past it. That's not true though. I can say it got *better*. But I still have the nightmares sometimes. I'm sorry it happened to you."

"Yeah, well, me too. But—half the refugees to the USA have been tortured. It's not like I'm alone. Thanks to you, it was over faster for me than a lot of others. That's twice I have something to thank you for, Vince."

"You'd do the same for me," he said. "For anyone."

She nodded. "I would."

"You ready for today?"

"No. But I'll be there. In that seat, piloting this heli."

"It probably will be a bridge too far in your career, Deirdre."

"I know." She looked around. "Is that a head?"

"Yep. There's a restroom in this thing. Big ol' luxury choppers, what can you say."

"Cool."

She went to the door of the little toilet and sink booth, like something in a 747, and he looked again at the GPS screen…

Shortly before nine that overcast morning, Mac Colls pulled the big dark-blue Buick up in the alley, parking next to a dumpster, behind Flesky's green Chevy Malibu. Flesky popped the trunk.

"We're running a little late," Mac said, turning off the engine and getting out. The alley smelled of last night's Chinese food leavings. "Come on, let's do this. Get the kid out and ready."

They were in an alley a block from Central Police Station 305, in the Third District of Washington D.C. There was room here to operate—it had all been scouted out. The spot was a wide place in the alley behind a Chinese restaurant and a small weight-lifting gym. The alley ran between two side streets.

"Get out, kid, and stay close," Buster said.

"I'm not a kid," Shaun said, opening the door. Except for asking for a piss break, it was the first thing he'd said since the drive from Ostrovsky House. They got out, Buster leveling the gun at Shaun across the top of the car. "Get to the front of the car, slow," Buster said. "Ain't no one around to see me shoot you, so don't make me do it."

"This whole thing is a lie," Shaun said, walking to the front of the car. "The vest is real and you guys aren't. You're just liars. You probably don't even believe half of Gustafson's bullshit. You just want to feel important."

"You get that from Bobby Destry?" Mac said, chuckling, as

Shaun came to the open trunk of the Chevy. "You know what happened to him? He's dead. We executed him."

"I don't believe anything you say, except," Shaun's voice was flat, almost monotone, but he was breathing hard and his fists were clenched, "I do believe you'd shoot me." He turned to look at Buster coming over with gun in hand. "Because you're the kind of guys who shoot people in the back."

"Okay, so you're not only a deserter," Buster said, "you're a traitor. You talk like a traitor to your people. Infected by the lies of the Jew agents."

Flesky, a gangly Russian with a bald head and a full blond beard, was taking the heavy explosive vest from the trunk. "Ve be so keer-ful vis zis." He had an atrocious accent. Another fucking immigrant, white or not, in Mac's view.

Then Buster said, "Who's that?" He nodded toward the west end of the alley, where a black sedan, probably a Crown Victoria, was pulling up in the street, blocking the alley egress. "That our people?" he asked nervously.

The car sat there. A man in dark glasses watched them—then drove on.

Mac's mouth had gone dry. "Nah, that's not us. But—it's nothing. Must've been sitting in traffic for a minute. Let's get the vest on him."

Buster was still looking toward the egress of the alley, frowning—and Shaun Adler saw his chance. He bolted toward the street, running past Mac—who stuck his boot out, catching Shaun's back foot. The young man went sprawling, cursing to himself. Then he scrambled to his feet—but Mac grabbed him, spun him around, and punched him glancingly in the jaw.

"Ow—*fuck!*" Shaun blurted, staggering back against the grill of the Buick.

"Okay, do that again, I'll shoot you in the nuts!" Buster snarled, pointing the gun at Shaun's groin.

"You're going to blow me the fuck up!" Shaun yelled, clutching his face. "What difference does it make!"

Mac pulled his Glock but he raised a hand, palm outward, and tried to talk in a calming voice. "Shaun, chill out, the vest isn't real! It's to keep them busy wondering, is all."

"There's that car again!" Buster said, pointing now at the east end of the alley.

Mac turned and saw the Crown Vic again, this time at the other end of the alley. He looked toward the east end. There was another black car there.

"Fuck! It's the feds!"

Shaun bolted again, with remarkable speed, running toward the closer car to the east, where an Asian-looking guy in a suit got out, gun in one hand, waving a badge with the other. "Drop your weapons! FBI!"

Shaun waved his arms. "Don't shoot me, I'm their prisoner, don't shoot!"

"Get down!" yelled the fed.

Shaun threw himself flat.

Mac turned to look toward the other end of the alley—and saw a large black man, suit, sunglasses, with gun and badge, coming at them from the other car.

"Drop your weapons!" the black fed yelled.

"Fuck this!" Mac said, and fired at the black guy.

He missed and the black cop returned fire. A corner of Buster's head exploded with a round and he fell as Flesky shrieked and ran, still mindlessly holding the explosive vest.

"No-no, *nyet*, don't shoot, this will explode!" Flesky yelled, running toward the east end of the alley.

Mac jumped up and fired at the black guy, who was still running at them, his bullet cutting at the agent's side. The fed grimaced but didn't stop, and fired back—and Mac felt something slam into his chest just below his collar bone.

A flash of red consumed his vision and he was whirling, falling, squeezing off a shot that smacked off the Buick's grill...

There was another gunshot and Flesky yelled in pain.

A roaring filled Mac's ears. He couldn't see...

Then the roaring receded, and he felt as if he were going down a drain, like all his blood was draining away into the earth. With an effort, he opened his eyes and saw two faces looking down at him—one was the Asian fed, frowning. The other was Shaun, standing behind him, eyes wide, ogling down at Mac. The black fed joined them, clutching his bleeding side. Somewhere a siren was wailing.

"He still with us, Richie?" asked the black fed.

"He's still alive, James," the Asian-looking guy said. "But maybe not long..."

Mac wanted to get out his phone and try to press the number code to explode the vest. But he couldn't lift his arms. There was no strength in them. He had just enough strength to speak. "It's coming... Firepower... Firepower is coming. You... are..."

The words died in his mouth, then, choked by rising blood. But before he died, he did have one last thought. *They're too late... too late to stop us...*

CHAPTER SIXTEEN

It was 9:25 a.m. and the H225 rotorcraft helicopter was skimming the rooftops, sliding in over Washington D.C. It flew as low as Deirdre dared to fly it to stay under the radar. She was flying so low, sometimes she had to pull it quickly, forty feet up, to keep from hitting power lines.

Vince had pushed the M134 Dillon forward on its tracks, locking it in place so its heavy-duty titanium muzzle was jutting out the open hatch. He was standing behind this modern, electrically operated Gatling, hands on the big machine gun's controls, a heavy black safety belt around his waist stretching to a bolt that the Brethren had installed in the starboard bulkhead behind him. A damp wind whistled through the open hatch.

"You know the Air Force is going to scramble jets, gunships, whatever, to come after us, because I'm not answering the radio," Deirdre shouted over the roar of the rotors and the wind.

"I'm still hoping you can get away without them identifying you," Vince shouted back.

"My fingerprints are all over this thing! And Bobby's probably going to have to testify, Vince! I don't want him to perjure himself."

Vince's mind was more focused on the immediate challenge. They'd just had word from Gus Gresley that the senators and a large crowd were gathered at the Lincoln Memorial—but some of Chang and Deirdre's allies at the FBI had finally decided to risk getting fired; they'd gotten through to organizers and the presentation was to be cancelled. Someone was on the stage right now, making an announcement to the four hundred people already gathered…

Too little too late, Vince thought. The crowd was already there—and so was the H225 heli now, as it soared in over the long narrow reflecting pool in front of the Lincoln Memorial, low enough that its rotors were making waves. A crowd was gathered in front of the steps leading up to the statue of Lincoln, while on the steps, near a portable podium, stood a group of men and women, who'd been ready to speak to the crowd through the PA system set up on either side. Television cameras were ready; microphones were propped up…

But a man in a braided police uniform was on the podium, waving his arms, telling them, Vince presumed, that the event was cancelled. The fancy-dressed people behind him were now hurrying away… Police were coming up from their cars, directing the crowd…

Maybe it had been stopped in time. Maybe what Vince had planned wouldn't be necessary.

He was scanning the vehicles coming to the streets beside the open area near the Lincoln Memorial…

There—a caravan of large delivery trucks, painted with fake logos on the sides: George Washington Laundry Service, Jefferson Davis Deliveries Inc., and four more; six rebuilt 46-foot delivery trucks with stolen plates, driving from two sides up the access streets. Pulling up, three on the north side, three on the south. Men in Brethren uniforms jumped out of the cabs, ran to open the trailer doors, releasing the militia assassins. They came piling out, guns in hand.

They were all wearing paramilitary togs, which Vince figured to be a big mistake on Gustafson's part. "The General" wanted to keep up his façade, his facsimile of an army—it was all about his vanity. But it made the gunmen visually easy to separate out from the non-militia. It made them targets.

Already, uniformed cops were turning toward the men jumping out of the backs of the trucks. But the Brethren began firing their weapons; AKs and AR-15s, fired toward the cops and the crowd.

Gritting his teeth in fury, Vince saw two cops falling under the onslaught and several people in the dispersing crowd stumbling, going to their knees, hit by the Germanic Brethren.

"Thirty degrees right, tilt to starboard!" Vince roared as the helicopter flew up to the green in front of the memorial. Deirdre tilted the H225, giving Vince a downward firing angle. He felt the safety harness holding him in place tighten.

Vince opened up, the big gun thundering, shivering in his hands, the 7.62 x 51mm rounds cracking down into the phalanx of oncoming militia gunmen sprinting across the grassy sward on the right. The strafe was chewing up a dozen armed Brethren, and a dozen more, so that they danced grotesquely in place as the bullets tore into them… ripping up flesh and sod… The cops were firing at the Brethren too, and so were FBI and Home Security agents, just arriving…

Too little too late…

"Come around the memorial building, sharp as you can!" Vince shouted, ceasing fire. "Head southeast, tilt down when we're parallel with those other trucks!"

"Roger that!" Deirdre circled the chopper over the white marble memorial building, came back to the line of trucks on the south side. Men were still jumping out of the trucks on that side—they were moving into action a little more slowly than those on the north side—and Vince fired directly down into the trucks, the rounds pocking through the thin metal, striking the engines, igniting gas tanks, tearing into men climbing out. Flames gushed up and pieces of truck flew and smashed into Brethren already on the ground.

Vince fired another long strafe at a large group of gunmen running through the line of steel posts toward the memorial steps. His rounds gashed into them, splashing blood on the green lawn. He was careful not to direct fire in a way that would risk the crowd or the cops.

A few more people in the fleeing crowd had fallen under bullets fired from the domestic terrorists, but now—as Vince had hoped—the Brethren had spotted the heli, were turning, firing up at him and Deirdre. Bullets cracked off the hull; windows spiderwebbed, and the windshield shattered on one side. At least they weren't shooting at the crowd.

Vince glanced over, saw that Deirdre seemed unhurt. She was ignoring the enemy gunfire and steadily controlling the helicopter. He had admired her before; he admired her even more now.

"Swing back around to the north side!" he called. "Head northwest, tilt for fire!"

"Copy that!" she yelled, her voice barely audible over the rushing wind coming through the shattered windshield. She circled the chopper back, heading west toward the memorial once more. Vince spotted more cop cars arriving.

Another strafing run, Vince targeting both the militia trucks and the Brethren on the lawn; some of the Brethren had dropped their guns and were running away to the north.

Vince fired another long burst, tracing it across the ragged line of domestic terrorists. Some of them returned fire, bullets cracking through the door around him and smacking into the bulkhead as he hammered at them; some virtually exploded with the impacts as they were hit by several big rounds apiece. Blood splashed; dirt geysered up. The trucks began to explode as he swiveled the gun to fire at them.

"Cut due north, then circle back south, tight as you can!" he shouted.

She shouted something unintelligible in response and veered due north. He glanced at her, saw she was talking into her headset; probably reporting who she was, saying she was with the FBI. Even giving her badge number. She wasn't authorized for any of what they were doing up here, but it gave the authorities on the ground around the memorial a chance to think, maybe preventing some panicky officers from opening fire on the heli.

Vince braced against inertia, gripping the machine gun, as Deirdre swung the helicopter tightly around, its engines screaming, militia bullets cracking by from behind. He was almost pulled from his two-handed grip on the M134 by the powerful gravitational torque as they came around to the south; then they straightened out, passing through smoke from the burning trucks below, and he yelled, "Tilt to starboard!"

She tilted and he aimed carefully, his downward fire cutting through a group of thirty more domestic terrorists who were running in all directions, some toward the memorial, some toward the crowd, others looking for cover. He fired in lethal bursts, ripping them apart like a mad surgeon.

Then he ceased fire as they passed over the crowd. Once past the crowd he opened up again, backing up the fire from the cops who were shooting at the last of the crowd of Germanic Brethren near the burning line of trucks on the south side…

The rounds tore through the militiamen, cutting them down, and then as the heli flew through the smoke from the trucks on the south side, he saw another dozen Brethren running through the walkway, away from the memorial, some of them throwing their weapons aside, desperately trying to escape.

"Go to hell, assholes," he said, remembering the innocents they'd cut down in the crowd at the memorial. He shouted, "Veer to port, thirty degrees, slight tilt for fire!"

"Roger!"

She turned the heli and he opened fire in short bursts, picking off the fleeing Brethren. Maybe one or two got through alive—more police were arriving to sweep them up.

Vince stopped firing, not wanting to risk hitting the cops. The surviving Brethren dropped their weapons and raised their hands.

And then the chopper flew on over them.

"Exfil!" Vince shouted. "Nothing more we can do here!"

"Glad to hear it!" she yelled. They had picked a landing zone: the southeast corner of Spirit of Justice Park at D Street and New Jersey Avenue, about forty blocks away. Not far in the fast heli. A minute, and they were approaching the park.

"Slowing for landing!" she yelled. The helicopter swung in a circle, slowing, over the park.

Vince held onto the stanchion and waited as Deirdre landed the helicopter at the southeast corner of the park. It was a bumpy landing because it was a hasty one. She had to get the chopper down as quickly as possible.

Then they were down, the engine shut off, the rotors slowing; Deirdre getting out of her seat, removing her helmet.

Vince unhooked the restraining harness and jumped out through the hatch onto the grassy lawn. He saw a security guard yelling at them from some distance off and a few people staring from beside an information kiosk, but no one was close enough to get a good look at him.

He took stock. His ears were ringing from firing the big machine gun, but he didn't seem to have been hit by the groundfire. He had the little pack on his back, with the Desert Eagle and ammo in it, along with several hand grenades, the flashlight and his knife. He had ditched his phone—he didn't want to be traced.

Deirdre stepped down beside him. She was breathing hard, looking around at the park as if it were the strangest sight she'd ever seen. "Oh God. That was insane."

"I saw you were on the radio," he said. "You told them who you were?"

"Yes. I took an oath. I've already broken it helping you, Vince. I can't keep this up. I'm not going to be a fugitive."

"Maybe they'll see you didn't have much choice because no one was listening to us. We saved a lot of lives today. Hundreds."

"And we took a lot of lives."

"No one who didn't need killing," Vince said.

"You've got to get out of here," she said. She took his hand and looked into his eyes. "You need to get to the metro."

He looked at her—and wanted to tell her a lot of things. He wanted to say they might try to see one another, sometime; that this could all blow over and it'd be okay…

But he knew that wasn't going to happen. He couldn't risk her.

"Deirdre—thank you. I'm sorry about what you're going to go through now."

"Just remember this, Vince. If I'm not under arrest, in ten days I'll be at Pomander Park, on the Potomac, in Alexandria. At noon."

This offer to meet surprised Vince. He'd been resigned to never seeing Deirdre again. "Okay. I'll be there if I can."

She nodded. "Maybe I'll have that information about Angel Lopez. You know, I can't guarantee I won't tell the Bureau who was with me in this heli. It depends on if they put me under oath."

"They probably will. They'll want to know who the vigilante is. And anyway—there are a lot of surviving Brethren from up at Wolf Base who know who I am. They'll tell them. They'll tell some lies, too, of course. But—don't hold back. No point in it." He noticed the security guard hurrying toward them, one hand on his gun. "Guard's coming. Gotta go. Good luck, Deirdre."

He made himself drop her hand and turn away.

Then he jogged off, under the slowly whirling rotors, putting the helicopter between him and the security guard.

Vince got to the street, then turned left and strode quickly off. The Capitol South Metro Station was close by. He couldn't stay and explain himself to the authorities. He had more business to take care of with the Brethren. If he left it to the FBI, by the time they got organized to do something about it, chances were,

Gustafson would escape. And even if the feds did get there on time, they'd arrest Gustafson, instead of killing him. He might be able to deny his connection to the attack—he'd likely covered his tracks pretty well. They might not take him into custody. So "the General" would escape.

Remembering the people struck dead by militia bullets at the memorial, right under the calm, marble-carven eyes of Abraham Lincoln, Vince simply could not allow Gustafson to escape punishment.

In a few minutes he was striding quickly along a passenger boarding dock of the subway. He had paid his metro fare as sirens from emergency vehicles roared by, and people around him asked one another what was going on. A woman said something about seeing a helicopter landing in the park, right over there...

Now, Vince stepped through the doors of the train and sat down, keeping himself looking serene as possible. He half expected the train to be stopped and searched by the police. But it pulled out of the station and rushed through the tunnels.

He had chaos on his side: the Brethren's attack on the memorial, the carnage left by the rogue machine-gunner on the heli, the strange helicopter landing in the park, Chang dealing with finding Shaun Adler, and a host of cops and Homeland Security arrayed around the Pentagon and the Joint Chiefs, thanks to Gus Gresley. Then there were people who had to be rushed to hospitals, there were militiamen to interrogate, and the bodies of many more Brethren shot to pieces near the memorial. All that had to be dealt with—and all of it was going to be overwhelming the local police for a good long while. They likely had no clear description of the helicopter gunman.

Unnoticed by police, Vince headed toward the state line, and Alexandria.

And to the first of many buses he planned to take on his way to a certain town in West Virginia…

CHAPTER SEVENTEEN

The rain came and went, and came again toward the middle of the next morning as the semitruck roared through the mountains.

"Sure glad to have the company, seeing as I got to drive across two states," said Dutch. That's what he said people called him, Dutch, because his family was from Holland. He was a ginger-haired fellow with a clipped red beard, lots of freckles and lots of forehead revealed by a receding hairline. Vince liked the affable trucker. He had freckles on his thick forearms and even the back of his big hands as he manhandled the heavy black steering wheel.

Vince had found that changing buses was going to take too long. He didn't want to rent a car in case the feds had an alert for him, so early that morning, a hundred miles east of Alexandria, Virginia, he'd gotten out of a bus near a truck stop. He'd spotted half a dozen eighteen-wheelers in the parking lot and chatted with the drivers outside. Hoping for a ride going his way, Vince came across Dutch, the friendliest of the lot.

Dutch had been in the army, in Iraq—his tattoo had given Vince a conversation starter—and when he heard Vince was a former Ranger, Dutch's interest perked up. He'd asked a few questions to see if the story was bullshit, of course. Lots of guys claimed to be ex Special Forces who weren't. But he was soon convinced. Vince didn't mention his service in Delta Force. Neither Delta Force nor the CIA encouraged discussing it.

"I tell you what," said Dutch as they screeched around a turn in the mountain highway, "I admire you re-enlisting as much as you did. Four years over there was enough for me. My left arm and ear all fucked up from an IED, my buddy killed…" He shook his head. "But the service helped me get a loan to buy this truck."

"You like being a wildcatter?" Vince asked. "Not tempted to just join a big company and let them worry about maintaining the rig?"

"Sometimes, because maintenance is a headache for sure! And I got to take a lot of work to make ends meet. Got to drive all the way across the country, some trips. I'd like to work regionally, round the Carolinas, where I live, so's I can get married. I got a girl, but…" He shook his head. "Don't know if I can ask her to put up with me being gone so much. Now, if I joined up with a company, I would always be getting paid. Right now, I got an empty trailer, coming home. Couldn't find anything to haul back…"

Vince could feel the trailer's emptiness when they took the curves. Dutch liked to push his speed to the limit, and without much drag the empty trailer swung out on the curves in a way that made Vince nervous. His own nervousness amused him. Bullets had come zinging past his skull like hail, recently, and he was worried about a trucking accident? Human nature. All the same he had a tendency to clutch at a grip bar atop the door when they whipped around a tight curve.

Dutch reached out and turned on the radio. "...earlier reports of two hundred domestic terrorists killed at the Lincoln Memorial were false. DCPD has just given us a count on eighty-eight killed, twelve seriously wounded, fourteen arrested unhurt or with non-life-threatening injuries. Police believe six others may have escaped. Seven people, targeted by the terrorists, are dead as a result of the terrorist attack, including one police officer, with eight more hospitalized... The vigilante who used a machine gun to stop the attack has been tentatively identified as—"

"That sure was a helluva thing," Vince said, hoping to cover up the mention of his name. He had given his name to Dutch as Vince. There were a lot of Vincents around. But the media would probably mention his background, including the Rangers. "I heard a report on someone's laptop, the guy sitting next to me on the bus. Lot of those American Nazis killed, all at once. Wild."

"Yeah, it was that."

The radio news segment ended, replaced by a country singer, something about trucks.

Dutch was frowning now, as if puzzling. But he said, "Hell, I don't think anybody but their mamas will miss them Nazi assholes. But it's sure too bad that fella couldn't have told somebody, they could have called that thing off. Then no innocents would've gotten killed."

Vince nodded dourly. "Yeah. It's too bad." He shrugged. "I understand he and an FBI agent tried. There was a lot of confusion. No one was listening. I heard."

Dutch glanced at him, still looking bemused. "You said you were coming from the D.C. area?"

"Alexandria."

"And you're headed to Wersted? You got family there?"

"No, some business to finish."

Dutch nodded. "Yeah, I don't know why anybody'd go to that town unless they have to. Lot of crooks there. Russian mafia came in, bought up the town. It's mostly whorehouses and crooked gambling now." He hesitated, then said, "I hope that doesn't offend you. Maybe you got work there. Friends and stuff."

"Nope, no friends there. Only work I have there is… unpaid. Just some old business to take care of. I hope to be in and out the same day."

"Well, I can get you close…"

They drove on, slowing for small towns, stopping for diesel once. Vince got a cup of coffee from the little convenience store at the gas station and heard people discussing the terror attack in Washington. It was big national news, and his name was out there, now. He wondered if he should turn himself in—if he survived his visit to Wersted. When the other shoppers glanced at him, he turned away, not sure if his picture was on the news yet.

He climbed back up into the Kenworth tractor-cab beside Dutch, and they headed out. Two hours more and they stopped for lunch in a West Virginia mountain town—Vince never did catch the name of it.

They ate lunch, Vince insisting on paying—he had more than enough cash on him—and they exchanged stories about service in Iraq.

Afterwards Vince went to a convenience store and bought a burner phone. Dutch was using the restaurant bathroom, so Vince went to the tractor-cab and sat on the mounting step under the door on the passenger side, thinking about Deirdre and the people Gustafson's followers had managed to kill. Would he get to Gustafson in time?

And what about Rose Destry and Bobby? Were they safe? Maybe it was time to call them. He set up the burner phone, used it to call Rose Destry.

"Vincent!" she said. "I almost didn't answer because it gave no number!"

"It's a burner phone, Rose. Where are you?"

"We're up in Connecticut. I've got some family up here."

"Did Bobby find the motorcycle where I left it? Still there?"

"Yes, this time of year people don't go up to Sullivan Rock. He found it and put it in the truck, brought it to the cabin. But it's yours, Vince. We want you to have it."

"Someday I'll take you up on that. Can I talk to him?"

"Sure. Listen, Vince—thank you for bringing my boy home."

"My pleasure, Rose."

Bobby came on the line. "Vince! Hey, man! I got a call from Shaun!"

"He's okay?"

"Yeah—he's testifying. They put him up in a nice hotel. He's turning evidence against the Brethren. They're gonna have to hide him somewhere afterwards…"

Vince heard Dutch coming back to the truck, going around to the other side. "Listen—I've got to go. I'll be in touch sometime."

"Vince—you keeping your head down?"

"Always. Take care of your mom for me."

He hung up, put the phone in his coat—and then sat listening to the voices coming from the other side of the truck.

"I saw how much money you had in that wallet when you

bought them snacks, man." A reedy male voice. Maybe a guy in his twenties. "You give me the money and you drive away and no one needs to get hurt. This gun's got hollow-point bullets. They'll fuck you up."

"Fuck you and your junkie friend," Dutch said.

Vince had left his pack locked in the truck. With his gun and knife in it. He shrugged and got up, walked around the front of the Kenworth.

He found two young men bracing Dutch who stood with his back to the tractor-cab. One of them was acned with long, greasy blond hair; the other, his face gaunt and pitted, had his head shorn. Both were skinny, dressed in baggy pants and t-shirts and open plaid shirts. Their eyes were sunken and the urgency in their body language said *opiate addicts*. Probably oxy heads; hillbilly heroin. The one with the greasy blond hair had a 9mm pistol in his hand.

The junky with the lank blond hair was saying, "You know what, 'Red', I can shoot you, and take your wallet, and drive off with your fucking truck and maybe sell whatever's in it, how'd that be?"

Striding toward them Vince said sharply, "Hey—point that at me!"

Startled, the gunman turned to Vince who was already stepping in, left hand gripping the gun barrel, pointing it up at the sky; his right pistoning out to rabbit-punch the junkie in the jaw. He felt bones break.

Vince jerked the gun from the junkie's hand and cracked him over the head with it, at the same time turning sideways to evade a slash from a buck knife wielded by the bald one. The first junky was folding over, out cold as Vince sank his fist in the second junkie's brisket. The bald guy doubled over and Vince cracked him over the head with the gun. He fell beside his friend.

Then, he and Dutch stood there a minute, contemplating the two men sprawled on the asphalt. "Well you sure didn't give me much to do, dammit, Vince," Dutch said, shaking his head.

Vince opened the pistol. There were three bullets in it. "Down to their last three bullets. But he could've killed you with them. The mystery is, how'd a couple of junkies not sell their gun to get their shit?"

"That would've happened sooner or later, if they lived long enough. I guess we should call the police?"

"You know what, let's not bother. Staties or the sheriff might keep us here for a week dealing with it."

"You got that right."

"We'll dump their weapons in the first river we see. Meanwhile…" He looked around, seeing that no one was watching. The semitruck blocked them from the view of the restaurant and store. "Let's drag these knuckleheads over there and drop them in that dumpster. They can figure out their lives from there…"

That's what they did. The two men were waking up, groaning when they were dumped in the big trash dumpster.

Without looking back, Vince and Dutch returned to the truck and got under way. They'd just slowed on a bridge over a river so Vince could toss the junkies' weapons over the railing, when Dutch said, "You were pretty quick to say we'd best leave the cops out of it. I guess I wasn't surprised."

"Yeah? Why's that?" Vince asked, rolling the window back up as the truck picked up speed.

"I wasn't sure till I saw you handle those two. A Ranger, sure, but that kind of efficiency—Lord!" He shook his head. "And you fit the description. I saw it on my phone when you were in that store. A former Army Ranger name of Vincent coming out of the D.C. area… You got money but for some reason you're hitching a ride. And—I could feel something was up. You're him."

"Okay," Vince said with a shrug. "That worry you?"

"Nope! Hell, you just saved my ass. And anyway—me and you are on the same side…" Dutch took his cell phone from a shirt pocket and passed it to him. "Turn that on, there."

Vince did. The phone showed a photograph of a smiling black woman, about thirty-five. She looked shy but happy.

"That's my girlfriend—my Shanna. Fuck them Nazis anyway."

Gustafson was pacing back and forth in the den of the Gustafson house, waiting for Dunsmuir to get back to him. Dunsmuir was to take him in the yacht, The Spirit of Purity, to the Cayman Islands, well away from the untidy aftermath of Operation Firepower. Normally he'd have flown there in the helicopter but that vile, treacherous thief Bellator had stolen it. Dunsmuir, Gustafson's hired yacht coxswain, was one of the Brethren and surely he must get back in touch soon. Or had the news from Washington sent him into hiding?

A log fire was burning in the massive gray stone fireplace; the rain was pattering on the windows. The place was cozy, with books and leathern chairs. A stein of German beer was going flat on the big oaken desk.

Yet Gustafson wanted badly to be away from this "safe house". The Russians had not confirmed that they would pick him up in the Caymans and take him to the dacha on the Black Sea as they'd promised, and many of the surviving Brethren were not returning his calls. A few from Wolf Base were said to be cooperating with the FBI. And certainly, that other treasonous worm Shaun Adler was spilling his guts, telling many a tale to the feds. Ostrovsky claimed that the safe house was entirely unknown to the Bureau—even to Dawson—and he was quite safe here. But Adler may have reported the whereabouts of the place.

A chilling thought came to him. Could Adler be in touch with... Bellator?

Still, Gustafson had some very capable men here, protecting him: Chaz Prosser, Henry Spellman, Dusty Folkson, Gunny Hansen, and two others. They were alert, well-armed, and this house was nearly a fortress in itself.

If only Dunsmuir would call him back...

He was troubled, his nerves jumping. Gustafson walked to the desk, picked up the stein, then put it down, the beer untasted.

The Operation. One attack had not carried out at all—the men lost their nerve; the suicide bomb never detonated, Flesky wounded and blathering to the feds, Adler escaped and cooperating with the FBI, Colls killed before he could carry out the Joint Chiefs attack. Buster killed. Then the slaughter of the Brethren at the Lincoln Memorial.

Gustafson went back and forth in his mind over whether he had achieved anything. They had killed a handful of the crowd. True, none of the senators had been killed—though they had been targeted. And almost all the Brethren had died or surrendered themselves. The Russians were satisfied—they didn't care who won or lost as long as there was more social chaos, disruptive violence and terror fomented within America.

But what was his next move? Perhaps the Sacred Cause would consider the dead Brethren to be martyrs. Certainly, when he regrouped with his people, in time, the next operation would be devastating to the liberals and Jews and their black minions…

A knock on the door. "Mr. Gustafson?"

It was Polly, with his dinner probably. "Yes, Polly?"

"Mr. Ostrovsky would like to speak to you!"

"Well—can he not come to me? I'm awaiting a very important call."

Ostrovsky came. He was wearing an old-fashioned scarlet smoking jacket, with yellow lapels, an ascot, tweed trousers, and slippers. He was smoking a Gauloises cigarette, which annoyed Gustafson. Though his own fortune derived from tobacco, he disliked second-hand smoke. A tall, pallid, bony gentleman of seventy with strangely red lips and deep-sunk rheumy blue eyes, Pieter Ostrovsky was a somewhat ghostly presence who engaged in long silences and sudden announcements.

It was his time for a sudden announcement. "Raoul, I'm afraid you must depart this very night," he said in his soft Russian accent.

"What? My boat is not yet confirmed…"

"I'm sure your man will confirm. If not, you can hire someone else. Go quickly to your yacht at Charleston."

"I need Dunsmuir to take the yacht out and I will take a separate boat out to it. Federal agents may be watching it."

"Your man Dawson surely is protecting you?"

"The Attorney General has taken a 'leave of absence' this

morning. He is expected to resign. Too much has come out…
He cannot help me."

"All the more reason you must depart. You have your men; you
have your Humvee. I am not equipped to protect you any further;
indeed, I am ordered not to. You know, this was supposed to be
my retirement, supervising this house. I did not expect anything
so… well, they did not tell me what to expect. But I have been
informed that this Shaun Adler has told them about *this very
house*. You must leave, almost immediately, and I must leave the
instant my chauffeur arrives. Pack what you have, tell your men,
and depart. I must insist. You would not want to anger the *Sluzhba
Vneshney Razvedki*. There will be just time for a cold collation in
the kitchen. Sliced beef, bread, and cheese, with coffee. Please
prepare yourself."

With that he blew a plume of smoke into the room and turned
away, leaving Gustafson staring after him, open-mouthed.

Vincent Bellator strode along, under the cloud-wracked night
sky, the asphalt of Greenville Road. He wore the service belt with
its holstered Desert Eagle, the sheathed knife, the SWIR night-
seeing goggles, a frag grenade, and two flashbangs.

It was about 8:00 p.m. He had been walking for two miles,
heading west from Wersted, West Virginia. Dutch had taken him
all the way to Wersted and he'd offered to drive him out to the
Ostrovsky house, but Vince didn't want to put him in danger.

Vince had few friends still living, and he didn't want to
lose another.

Greenville Road was gradually curving up a slope through a
forest of spruce intermixed with hemlock in the foothills of the

Adirondacks. Vince had seen not one vehicle on the road. Bats had flitted from the woods on either side, and an owl had called out, and he thought he'd seen the eyes of a bobcat glowing golden-green from a tree limb. But so far, except for a 747 droning high overhead, no sign of humanity.

But after another quarter mile he saw lights glimmering through the trees up ahead. One of them seemed to be headlights.

Vince stepped off the road, walked along the gravel siding close to the trees, ready to slip under cover.

He hurried now, jogging up the hill, one hand plucking the goggles up, putting them on. He kept the lenses flipped up for now. There was some light from the full moon and the occasional spangle of stars showing through the clouds.

Soon the road curved sharply to the north, dead-ending about a hundred feet in a short steel barrier. Vince stopped just before a gravel driveway, which headed west between a big overhanging oak and a group of beeches. It circled up beside a hulking gray-stone house. Looking through a tangle of shrubs and lowering tree branches, he could see the arching front entrance of the house, and a group of men, two of them loading luggage into the back of a black Humvee, probably the one that he'd seen driving away from Wolf Base.

There was a light fixture shining over the doorway, but he couldn't see the men clearly from here, mostly just their silhouettes. He could see the profiles of assault rifles on straps over the shoulders of three of the men.

There was another car there too, long and low, closer to the road—it was a limousine and its headlights were on. A tall, thin man, accompanied by a woman, hurried to the limo. No one opened the door for them. The tall man opened the back door, let the woman get in, then he slid in after her. The moment the door shut, the limousine started moving. The passenger side window was open and as Vince stepped into the shadowy brush, watching the limo drive by, he saw the tall man's face as the window was closing. Something about the shape of the eyes and the cheekbones made him think *Russian.*

A slight extra bulkiness to the limo's body prompted Vince to suspect it was armored. He hoped Gustafson wasn't in it. If he was, he could take the Humvee, if he lived to do that, and pursue the limo. Maybe force it off the road.

But there —as he turned back toward the house—wasn't that the distinct shape of Raoul "the General" Gustafson emerging?

CHAPTER EIGHTEEN

Vince flipped on the night-seeing goggles.

Through the unnatural green view of the goggles, the porch light's glare blocked out some of the scene, but he could make out Gustafson putting a small bag in the back of the Humvee. The General wore an overcoat. Definitely leaving. Another handful of seconds and Gustafson would have escaped.

He still might get away. Vince recognized three of the men with Gustafson from Wolf Base. They'd come in the day before Vince had departed—men from outlying Brethren units. All of them wore Brethren paramilitary uniforms. One of them, a lean man with a long face and a prow of a nose, was a former British paratrooper, Charles Prosser; liked to call himself Chaz. The broad-shouldered stocky guy with the buzzcut was Henry… something. Vincent hadn't heard his last name. Story was, he was ex-Navy Seal, investigated for murdering Taliban prisoners, and expelled from the service. Dusty Folkson, the tall one with the apish long arms, prognathous jaw, and blond hair tied behind his head, was formerly a Blackwater operative. Investigated for murdering Iraqi civilians. Said to be a Grand Wizard of the Mississippi KKK.

They were all experienced, dangerous men. And there were three more armed Brethren—one was Gunny Hansen. Vince didn't know the other two. This could be a tough nut to crack.

May as well cut to the chase, Vince thought. He took a grenade and a flashbang from his belt.

Stationing himself close against the oak, he pulled the pin on the flashbang, looked around the trunk of the tree—and tossed the flashbang through a gap in the foliage.

He'd put enough force in the throw to get it to the group of men at the door. He heard the *crack-whuff* of the pyrotechnic going off and caught the strobe of sudden intense white light from the corner of his eye. The men yelled, Gustafson loudest, as Vince pulled the pin on the fragmentation grenade, stepped out from the tree trunk, and threw it at the men stumbling around, cursing and clutching their eyes. He noticed Gustafson running clumsily back to the open front door. The three professionals—Chaz, Dusty and Henry—had enough experience to rush after Gustafson. The frag grenade exploded and the other three men shrieked as the shrapnel sliced through them. The explosion blew out the back tires of the Humvee and started a fire on its oily underside…

Vince was already drawing his Desert Eagle and—not wanting to be framed against the driveway—he forced his way through the brush to the left of the door. Branches stung his cheeks; thorns raked his knuckles. Then he was through, onto the lawn—just as the window to the left of the door shattered. An assault rifle burst, fired through the window, sliced by on his right—the shooter's eyesight was still somewhat compromised or Vince might well be dying right now.

Vince dodged right, sprinting hard to put the Humvee between himself and the house. He saw three men sprawled on the ground, two quite motionless, the third—Gunny Hansen--trying to crawl away. Probably dying.

The flames were licking up the heavy vehicle's chassis now, and smoke was billowing. Good cover. But the damn thing might blow up in his face in a second.

He kept running, bullets cracking behind him, toward the corner of the house. He saw a face in a window on the right side of the door and fired the Desert Eagle at it. The face vanished.

Did he hit the guy? Unlikely.

He got to the corner of the house, decided that outnumbered, he couldn't creep slowly along—they'd use the time to catch him between them.

So he kept sprinting, jumping over a garden bench, then a short hedge, coming around to the back yard. A landscaped garden stretched between him and a broad wooden porch that looked out on a small valley behind the house. Beyond the valley a slope rose up to join a steep wooded hill.

There were lounge chairs on the porch. On his left was a long window and he was relieved to see the curtains closed. He ducked under it, moved as quickly forward as he could in that awkward hunched-over position, past the windows. He straightened up just as a burly man stepped onto the porch, rifle in hand. The gunman had a buzzcut. Henry.

He and Vince saw one another at the same moment, but Vince's pistol was already leveled, while Henry's rifle wasn't raised to firing position yet. Vince had gotten here faster than Henry had expected—but Henry was wearing a Kevlar Vest.

Vince didn't let that stop him from firing at Henry's center-mass. The Desert Eagle boomed and the heavy .50 round knocked the militiaman off his feet. Vince doubted the bullet had penetrated the armor but now, crouching down again, Vince could see Henry sprawled under the middle railing of the porch. There was a space under the plank and the deck, and there was Henry, groaning, getting up to a sitting position, firing sloppily. The rifle bullets tore through the middle plank and cracked over Vince's head.

Vince was aiming right between Henry's outstretched legs. "Sorry, Henry," he said, as he squeezed the trigger.

Henry screamed as the .50 smashed into his groin, the powerful bullet wreaking havoc, shattering not only genitals but arteries and major veins.

Vince threw himself down as Henry, shrieking curses, chewed up the railing with the rest of his clip.

There was a click as the rifle came up empty and a sob from Henry as Vince stood up, took careful aim, and shot Henry through the head.

Taking a deep breath, Vince rushed to the wall between the window and the porch—as he expected, the window shattered as bullets sprayed through it. Broken glass flew past. The gunfire had brought Henry some back-up.

Vince had four rounds left in the pistol and not enough time to reload—not with two experienced soldiers hunting him. He clambered quickly over the porch railing and flattened against the wall.

Where would Chaz and Dusty go now? Probably one would be trying to keep his attention while the other flanked him.

Heart banging away, Vince looked to his right, back at the

northern corner of the house. No one visible yet. He heard foot-steps inside, someone moving from the window to the door onto the porch. The window on his right was broken, its curtain tattered. He leaned out a little, glanced through it. Saw no one.

Vince took the second flashbang from his belt, pulled the pin, and tossed it through the break in the window. The noise of its falling might make the shooter by the door look toward it.

Crack-whuff, the peripheral burst of light, and a man shouted, *"Bloody Hell!"* Chaz.

Vince turned toward the door—bullets smashed the glass of the big window beside the porch as Chaz, blinded but trying to keep Vince at bay, fired his rifle. Vince rushed to the door and fired through its broken window at the Brit. Chaz's head jerked and he staggered back.

Vince didn't see him fall because he had to throw himself to the left as bullets from the corner of the house cut past him. Vince hit the deck hard, rolled, got to one knee with the stone porch pillar between him and Dusty.

Luckily for Vince, Dusty Folkson was Blackwater-trained; just private "army", not as professional as the other two, and not as good a shot.

Vince heard the man's running feet—he was sprinting toward the porch, counting on the porch pillar to cover him.

He'll have his gun tilted toward the house, Vince thought, thinking of me being likely to shoot at him from up on the porch.

So Vince got up and jumped off the porch, turning in the air, landing and awkwardly trying to aim as Dusty got up on his feet. Vince fired, twice. And both times, firing off balance—he missed.

Dusty turned, spraying with the AR-15 burst setting as he

came, and Vince had only one bullet left in the Desert Eagle. As the bullets zinged off flagstones to his right, Vince let his professional calmness settle over him, and he aimed carefully—and blew a trench through the middle of Dusty's forehead.

Dusty went to his knees, twitched, and fell on his face.

Vince stood there a few seconds, getting his breath, his pulse hammering in his ears.

Then he heard a *creak*, a noise from the room on the other side of the window, turned to see Gustafson raising a Glock to fire at him through the window. Vince spun and threw himself at the foot of the porch, the Glock cracking as he went.

He hit the ground hard and gasped for air as he got to his feet. He rushed up the steps to the wall beside the door, holstering the Desert Eagle and unsheathing the knife.

"You Judas to all that is holy!" Gustafson bellowed, rushing up to the door and firing through. The General had the wrong idea of where Vince was.

Knife in hand, Vince edged closer to the doorframe. He looked down and saw a large shard of glass from the door lying on the deck. He reached, picked it up, and tossed it toward the big shrub close to the stone walkway, from the porch steps.

The glass tinkled there, and Gustafson thrust his arm through the door's broken window, extending the Glock to fire at the shrub.

Vince swung the knife hard and fast so the blade pierced to the hilt through Gustafson's extended arm, cutting between the radius and ulna. The General screamed as blood spurted from his arm and Vince twisted the knife so that Gustafson would lose control of his hand.

The gun fell from his twitching fingers.

Vince withdrew the knife and Gustafson wrenched his arm back into the house. Vince used the toe of his boot to pull the gun toward him—he wasn't sure that Gustafson didn't have a second gun. He wiped the combat knife on his belt and sheathed it, picked up the Glock, hearing Gustafson's retreating footsteps. No time to load the Desert Eagle.

Stepping to the door, Vince saw Gustafson running crookedly past Chaz Prosser's body. He was heading toward a doorway, clutching his arm and sobbing.

Vince opened the door and stepped through, striding after Gustafson.

"Herr Professor!" Vince yelled. "Where you going? You wanted firepower—I got some for you! Come on back and take down the Judas!"

Vince got to the doorway, saw Gustafson running through a sort of parlor and through another door.

Vince followed and saw Gustafson running out onto the front porch. Raoul Gustafson stumbled on the stairs and fell on the ground between the porch and the burning Humvee, yelling with pain as he hit his wounded arm on the ground. He writhed about, cursing, then got awkwardly to his feet and started past the car, coughing from the smoke. He walked past the body of Gunny Hansen, not even glancing down.

"*Herr Oberstgeneral!*" Vince shouted in his freshman German. "Achtung! Stop or I'll shoot you in *der hintern!*"

The General staggered onward.

Vince followed him out to the driveway and then fired the Glock in the ground between Gustafson's feet.

Swaying, the General stopped in mid-stride. Then he turned to

Vince, composing his face for dignity, raising his chin. "I officially surrender to you!" he said. The light from the burning car played on his face, red as hell-flames.

"Do you really?" Vince said, stopping about ten feet away.

"You *must* take me prisoner," Gustafson said. "And turn me over to the authorities! You are a professional soldier. You are a man of conscience. You cannot shoot down an unarmed man."

"I can't?"

"Certainly not."

Vince chuckled. "Herr General—if the people your thugs murdered at the Lincoln Memorial had put up their arms and asked to surrender, what would have happened to them? Would your men have spared them?" He shook his head. "You know, one of the dead was a minister with four children. He was a veteran. Another one was a young woman right out of medical school. She was going to be an oncologist. She's dead now. And you *tortured* a friend of mine. And you're telling me I have to let you live? Fuck you. Raoul Gustafson, I sentence you to death for treason against the United States of America." He aimed the gun at Gustafson's belly.

Gustafson's eyes widened. "No—you're a civilized man!"

"I'll do this much for you," said Vince. "I'll give you this guy! And you can then—be armed."

"What?" Gustafson blinked at him, frowning, as if he hadn't heard right.

Vince took two long steps forward—and then tossed the Glock pistol at Gustafson's feet. "Go on, Raoul. It's loaded. Pick it up."

Gustafson stared—and then sneered. "Truly—you slaves of the Jews are imbeciles!"

He reached down, scooped up the gun…as Vince unsheathed his combat knife, stepped in close—intimately close—and stabbed it expertly between two ribs over Raoul Gustafson's heart.

The Glock fired as Gustafson convulsively squeezed the trigger, the bullet smacking into the gravel behind Vince…

Whimpering, Gustafson stared into Vince's eyes.

"Gustafson," Vince said, "you're about to find out that Hell is real."

The leader of the Germanic Brethren slumped, his eyes glazing over.

Vince let him drop, tugging the knife free. He wiped the blade on the dead man's body and sheathed it. He stepped over the body and kept walking, heading down the driveway to Greenville Road. Dutch was waiting for him in his truck, down at a turnout on the highway.

Vince kept walking, emotionally drained, shaking a little as a light, cooling rain began to fall.

Then he saw headlights coming…

He stepped off the road and hid in the brush. A motorcade of federal cars arrived—and drove right past him. They hadn't seen him, it seemed. There was a black Crown Vic, two SWAT vans, and two other sedans. They swept on up the road.

What they found there should keep them busy for a while…

Vince returned to the road and continued on his way. The walk down to the highway seemed to take no time at all. His mind was lost in thoughts of Chris Destry and the dead at the Lincoln Memorial, and all the lies told on the internet.

And Deirdre…

* * *

232

A gray day in early November.

Vince rode the old trail-bike up into the nearly empty parking lot alongside the park. There was only one car there. A black Crown Vic.

So they're letting her drive the company vehicles, he thought. Things couldn't be too bad.

He parked the bike, pocketed the keys, and took off his motorcycle helmet. It was one of those black helmets with a tinted visor completely covering the rider's face. He could see her on a concrete bench overlooking the Potomac River. She was just sitting there, alone.

Any chance, he wondered, the feds were in the bushes, somewhere, watching. Was this a set-up? Would she do that to him?

No. She wouldn't.

Carrying the helmet, he crossed the broad swathe of grass, up to the asphalt walk.

Deirdre glanced over at him, damp wind fluttering her blond hair. He saw an inch of her natural brunette hair showing. She smiled wanly at him.

"You're letting your hair grow out natural," he said.

"I just dyed it for the Brethren," she said. She glanced behind at the parking lot. "You weren't followed?"

"Nope." He patted the visor of the helmet. "Got a cool disguise."

"So I see. Nice. You look like the bad guys in a Bond movie with that thing. Have a seat."

He sat beside her. The river smelled a bit rank. But she smelled like lavender soap. "How are they treating you, Agent Corlin?"

"I am not currently under arrest. I'm not supposed to leave the area. Probably coming over to Alexandria was against the rules. But I'm going right back."

"Politics involved?"

"An astute question. It's all about the politics. In a way, we're thought of as heroes—except for on certain conspiracy theory websites, where the Russian operatives are claiming that we were going to attack the crowd and the Brethren were going to stop us. And we were the ones who actually shot the people in the crowd and…"

He snorted and shook his head. Pushed the anger down. "The internet is about two-thirds babble."

"Almost no one takes these people seriously. But—I broke the rules. I'll at least be suspended. Probably have to resign. Might even do time—but actually I understand that if I'm convicted of helping a vigilante kill people, the president is going to pardon me and maybe even a certain Vincent Bellator, former Army Ranger."

"I'm not holding my breath." After a moment he added, "I did warn you, Deirdre…"

"I know you did."

They didn't speak for a minute. Both of them gazed at the syrupy flow of the Potomac. Then he prompted, "About Angel Lopez…"

She nodded. "I called a friend at the DEA. Lopez is now in the USA. He's chief of an Arizona branch of the cartel. Pushing meth and heroin. He's working with a guy named Danny Korski. This Korski is American-born Russian mafia. He's overseeing some kind of experimental partnership between the cartels and the Russian mob. He's got a small army around him."

"I see. *Where* in Arizona?"

"Kingman. But listen—you don't have to go there and try to kill this Lopez."

"He ordered the chopper to fire the missile."

"What missile?"

"The one that killed Chris Destry. And he's a major dirtbag. It'll be no loss to the world."

"No one will weep for Angel Lopez. But Vince—if you don't turn yourself in and let the process play out… you'll be a fugitive."

He shrugged. "I'm aware."

"Come back with me, Vince. We'll go into the Bureau together. You can surrender to Richie. Maybe get that pardon. You'll be treated with respect. Probably get an ankle bracelet but…"

Vince shook his head. "Cannot do it. This isn't finished yet."

"Listen…"

He shook his head. "I can't. I'm feeling like things are going to work out for you. I feel good about that. But I don't feel like they'd work out for me. And I need to take care of this. I promised Chris when I buried his hand."

"You did what?"

"His hand got shot off and I promised him I'd bury it under the cabin porch and… it's a long story, Deirdre."

"Vince." She reached out and put her hand on his. "Come with me. We'll take good care of you."

He turned his hand over and clasped hers, gave it a gentle squeeze. Then he let go of it and stood up. "I can't. But I hope to God I live to see you again."

She stood up, put her hands on his face, stood on tiptoe—and kissed him. It was a short kiss but it lit him up inside.

He stepped back, suddenly breathing hard. "That's not fair."

"Can't blame a girl for trying. Anyway—I promised myself I'd kiss you at least once."

He smiled and turned away while he still could. He strode quickly across the grass, putting on the helmet as he went.

He almost went back to her when he was nearly at the motorcycle. But—he'd promised Chris, when he'd buried his hand…

Vince got on the Harley, started it up, swung it around and rode away from the park.

He headed down the access road, a half mile, to where the big Kenworth truck was waiting for him. Dutch stood by the ramp at the rear of the trailer, beside the open rear doors.

Vince slowed, and then rode up the ramp, right up into the empty space, just big enough for the Harley, behind the boxes of wide-screen TVs. He turned off the engine, made sure the bike was secured in place, and then went down the ramp.

"She confirmed it—Lopez is in Arizona," he said.

He helped put the ramp up, and they walked up to the tractor-cab. They both climbed in, Dutch getting into the driver's seat.

Dutch started the truck as Vince took off the motorcycle helmet.

Dutch drove toward the freeway and within half an hour they were barreling along, a little above the speed limit, going west.